# The Box In The Attic & Other Stories by AM Burrage

Alfred McLelland Burrage was born in Hillingdon, Middlesex on 1st July, 1889. His father and uncle were both writers, primarily of boy's fiction, and by age 16 AM Burrage had joined them. The young man had ambitions to write for the adult market too. The money was better and so was his writing.

From 1890 to 1914, prior to the mainstream appeal of cinema and radio the printed word, mainly in magazines, was the foremost mass entertainment. AM Burrage quickly became a master of the market publishing his stories regularly across a number of publications.

By the start of the Great War Burrage was well established but in 1916 he was conscripted to fight on the Western Front. He continued to write during these years documenting his experiences in the classic book War is War by Ex-Private X.

For the remainder of his life Burrage was rarely printed in book form but continued to write and be published on a prodigious scale in magazines and newspapers. In this volume we concentrate on his supernatural stories which are, by common consent, some of the best ever written. Succinct yet full of character each reveals a twist and a flavour that is unsettling…..sometimes menacing….always disturbing.

There are many other volumes available in this series together with a number of audiobooks. All are available from iTunes, Amazon and other fine digital stores.

## Table Of Contents

### The Box in the Attic

He crouched in a comer of the room, his heart thumping like the piston of an engine, wondering if the footfalls would pass the door.

He was sick with terror. He promised himself and God—in Whom on ordinary occasions he professed a scornful disbelief—that if he could get safely out of that house he would go empty-handed and never 'go crooked' again.

He had made such promises before in other and less desperate circumstances; he had never tried to keep them.

The footfalls paused. The handle of the door clicked. A light sprang up in the comer and there was the momentary vision of a man standing in the doorway, holding up an oil reading lamp. A voice spoke.

'I have always heard that it is dangerous to look for a burglar with a light, but I am fatalist enough to be careless in such matters. Come over here and let's have a look at you. And don't try any nonsense.'

The voice was hard and cold but scarcely forbidding. There was not the least note of anger in it. Charles Plummer came out of the comer where he had been crouching and swayed as he walked. His fingers were working and twittering as if they played on a musical instrument.

'Oh, you're wearing a mask,' said the man with the lamp. 'Better have it off.'

The act of removing the crepe took time, for Plummer had small command of his hands. His captor eyed him critically.

'H'm,' he said, 'I don't wonder you wore it. You should wear one always and spare the feelings of your neighbours. However, perhaps you had better not resume it now. I am about to take the liberty of going through your pockets, so perhaps you had better put up your hands. I shan't trouble to warn you not to attempt anything foolish, for obviously you haven't the courage left to crack a flea.'

And the speaker calmly laid down the lamp upon a table and went toward his unbidden guest.

Plummer, regarding him out of the comers of his frightened eyes, saw him to be a tall, wiry man of fifty or over. His hair was grey and plentiful but cut very close. His face was white and very thin, with straight lips fitting tightly over prominent front teeth. His eyes were deep-set, and the whole aspect of his face was ominously like that of a death's head.

Yet there was no suggestion of weakness or sickness about the man. His movements hinted at great physical strength, and the unstudied calmness of his demeanour suggested certain reserve forces which were available when required.

He went through the youth's pockets with method and precision, replacing most of what he found and making occasional comments.

'What's this? Lemon drops? So you still eat sweets? You wouldn't if you knew what some cheap lemon drops are made of. What on earth—oh, I see! Catalogue of motorcycles. Of course, you've got a motorcycle. Or you thought of getting one at my expense.'

He pulled out a small pistol which he thrust contemptuously into his own pocket.

'What were you going to do with that pea shooter? Try to frighten somebody if you got caught? Or shoot somebody? But you didn't try either with me, did you? And now I think we'd better continue our pleasant little talk in the library, where there's a fire.'

All this time Charles Plummer had not spoken, and now he stood looking stupidly and interrogatively at his captor.

'Go on!' said the latter sharply, with a slight show of impatience. 'Go through that door in front of me.'

Plummer obeyed and found himself in a large square hall. Then he looked over his shoulder and spoke for the first time.

'Which way?' he asked hoarsely.

'Over there—the second door. Go straight in. I shall be following.' Plummer entered and found himself in a room which, apart from a large table, two small tables and some chairs, seemed to be furnished entirely with books. He had never before seen so many books in one room, for they covered every bit of wall space, and two short stepladders leaned against the shelves.

'Sit down,' said the older man. 'I think you'll find that chair pretty comfortable. Now we can talk. To begin with I must ask you a few questions. I need not impress on you the advisability of answering them truthfully. I have a keen ear for a lie, and on the truth rather than on the nature of your answers depends very largely the treatment which you may expect from me. I may as well tell you at once that it is very unlikely that I shall hand you over to the police.'

Plummer uttered a long, shuddering sigh.

'First we'll have your name?'

'Charles Plummer.'

'Ah! And age?'

'Twenty-two.'

'You come from Saylesville, I expect?'

'Yes, sir.'

'Are you in work? If so, where, and what wages are you getting?'

'Clovax Factory, sir. I gets sixteen a week.'

'I see. Do you happen to know my name or anything about me?'

'No, sir.'

'Then to what do I owe the pleasure of this visit?'

The captive gulped.

'I see the house when I was cyclin' by on a Sunday and I thought'

'I understand. You thought it would be nice and easy to rob. Well, I hate to hold the advantage of you, so I will tell you my name. It is Clongrail. In the village I believe I am known as the Professor. As a matter of fact I am a professor of science, but of what branch of science you need not be interested to know. My laboratory is at the back of the house. You need not tell me that this is your first attempt at the hazardous business of housebreaking and burglary'

'Never done it before, sir!' the youth broke in passionately. 'And I'll never do it again. I swear I won't.'

'No,' said Clongrail thoughtfully, 'I don't think you'll ever do it again, and I believe this is your first attempt. An older hand would not have been so clumsy, and he would have made a few preliminary inquiries.

'I don't fancy that many men who had first made a few discreet inquiries about me in the village would want to burgle me, although, to be sure, I am all alone in the house at night. I won't be so foolish as to ask you why you broke in. Of course, you wanted to steal something that you could sell for money Why did you want the money?'

Plummer hung his head.

'I dunno, sir,' he said sheepishly.

'Ah, but I do,' said the professor, and paused to light a cigarette. 'You are getting sixteen a week and it isn't enough. You want a motorcycle and a radio. You want to gamble and drink and have your fun with the girls. You have to steal to get all these things.'

Plummer flushed darkly.

'Perhaps *you'd* like to try livin' on sixteen a week,' he muttered.

'At your age I should have welcomed the opportunity. I was not earning so much until I was nearly thirty. At your age I was at the university. Don't think I had wealthy parents and influential friends. I was poor. I had a pipe, and just occasionally I was able to buy half an ounce of tobacco. Yet I was so dull-witted that it never occurred to me to steal.

'However, please don't suppose that I think any the less of you because you have chosen burglary as a career. I realize that burglars are a highly necessary factor in modem life.'

Plummer, suspecting that he was being jeered at, stared at the professor sulkily.

'I assure you,' continued that gentleman, 'that I am perfectly serious. A sudden dearth of burglars would be followed by a serious fall in business.

'Nobody would insure against them, and the companies would feel the pinch. Discharged policemen would swell the ranks of the unemployed. The manufacturers of firearms would no longer be able to sell revolvers to householders or to the gentlemen of your adopted profession. It would be nothing short of an industrial calamity.

'So, quite sincerely, I think you have chosen a useful and profitable calling, even if it is a little hazardous and precarious—provided, of course, that you have the true vocation.'

'I didn't say as I was goin' to keep on doin' it,' Plummer protested. 'I said as I was never going to do it again. '

Clongrail blew smoke rings and smiled.

'I don't doubt your present intentions,' he said, 'but they were probably different a little earlier in the evening. They would have been different now had you got away from this house with anything of value. And if you leave me none the worse for tonight's experience, as you very well may, who knows but you may change your mind again tomorrow?

'The fact that you are at present a very clumsy burglar need not deter you. Everybody must make a start, although in your profession, to be sure, it is a little expensive to learn by one's mistakes. Still, you might yet rise to great heights. Even in the best criminal circles they may speak of you with bated breath. You may yet hear yourself referred to as Gentleman Charlie. But the point is—have you the temperament?'

The captive stirred uncomfortably. He distrusted words of more than two syllables.

'I dunno know what you mean, sir,' he mumbled.

'Oh, I mean that I might excuse myself for launching a good burglar on the world, but I couldn't forgive myself for letting loose a failure. The greatest kindness one can do you is to put you to a test. You may fail, but it is best to know the truth at once.

'I know you are not quite a coward. If you were, you would never have dared to break into my house. But the question is, have you the nerve to carry on this profession? I am inclined to think not. When I caught you just now you were all in pieces. You had no resource at all, and about as much fight left in you as a wet biscuit. But we shall see, we shall see. You are to be congratulated on having fallen into the hands of a scientist.'

Terror came back into the youth's eyes. He had all the half superstitious dread of his kind for science and scientists.

'You ain't goin' to do nothin' with me!' he whined.

Clongrail leaned forward, and his eyes dilated a little.

'Do not let us be at cross-purposes, my friend,' he said smoothly. 'There need be no misunderstandings between us. I am going to do with you precisely as I choose. You selected for your first experiment a very lonely house which we two have to ourselves until my housekeeper arrives tomorrow morning. You may shout to your heart's content and attract no attention.

'But no, we are not entirely alone. I had a partner working with me until the day before yesterday, when he died—suddenly. How did he die? Well, that is no concern of anybody's. Perhaps—who knows?—he died of knowing too much. Perhaps I had a mind to take the undivided credit for a discovery which will presently stagger civilization. All that concerns you is that he is dead, and that for years he had been dabbling in a branch of science in which I confess to knowing nothing. I mean occult science.

'Hydeman seriously believed that for the first few nights after death *he would be able to resurrect himself for a few minutes at a time.*

'It may have been an idle boast. I cannot say. I must admit, however, to avoid any risk I have had the coffin and the body removed to an attic. The coffin will not be screwed down until tomorrow. I therefore propose to lock you in with it. If my late lamented friend and partner rises during the night you will be able to bear witness and report on the matter.

'He always had a confidential way of tapping one on the shoulder when he wanted to attract attention. Also, if your nerve will stand the strain of tonight's vigil I think we may take it that you may yet become an ornament to the craft of burglary. '

Charles Plummer sprang up with a cry.

'I ain't ' he began.

Clongrail rose more slowly and seized him by the wrists.

'You are,' he said quietly. 'Make no mistake about it. Don't get excited. You will need all your nervous force. I am afraid you will find it very dark in that attic. There is only one high dormer window, much too small for you to squeeze through. The lock and door will, I think, withstand any rough treatment you may give them.

'I am afraid you will have to spend your night on the floor. The bed is being occupied by the coffin, which your sense of touch will confirm when you go to explore the room. And now, if you are ready—or for that matter whether you are ready or not—I will conduct you to your quarters.'

Plummer screamed and began to struggle Suddenly, however, he stood rigid and on tiptoe, caught in an arm-lock.

'You see?' said Clongrail pleasantly. 'If you move now you break your arm. Don't try to kick me as we go upstairs. If you do you will find the consequences unpleasant. And now'—quick march.'

Sweating from every pore, shuddering and uttering sobbing protests, the wretched young man was propelled up three flights of stairs. On the top landing Clongrail thrust him against a door which snapped open under the impact. With one push Clongrail sent his victim flying headlong into the room, then he slammed and locked the door before the handle could be seized from the inside.

A series of piercing screams almost deafened the professor, but he turned unhesitatingly away and marched downstairs. The crashing of a door under the repeated onslaughts of fists and shoulders mingled with the screams and echoed throughout the house. The professor frowned, because he hated noise. The closing of the library door, however, shut most of it out.

It was quite light when, at seven o'clock on the following morning, Clongrail climbed to the top of the house and unlocked the attic. There was very little furniture in the room, but on the right of the door stood a dismantled bed, backed against the wall. On the bed rested an open box, long and rectangular. It had once contained a lawn tennis net and posts, but it was now quite empty.

Charles Plummer was squatting in one of the opposite corners of the room, playing some strange game he had devised with the pattern of the worn linoleum. He had been babbling and chuckling to himself, and now he looked up into Clongrail's face and laughed outright. He was quite mad.

Clongrail hastily closed and relocked the door, and went downstairs to ring up the local doctor.

'He would never have made a burglar,' thought the professor, as he took down the receiver.

## Portrait of an Unknown Lady

I had intended to be among the last of Frewland's guests to leave the flat that night, for I lived in another block only three doors away, in that part of Hampstead which marked the frontier line of Black King Plague's territory in the days when England was welcoming the second Charles.

It was his fault, or rather by his design, that I was quite the last, for I had already risen to make the rearguard of a procession of four to the door when I saw that the glass on the little table at my elbow had been replenished.

Now I hate wasting a perfectly good whisky and soda, even when I don't want it. A stern inner monitor whispers to me, 'Ah, laddie, laddie, you may need that one of these days!' Also I could see the design which had prompted the Hidden Hand to administer the dose. It was Frewland's way of detaining me until the others had gone.

He re-entered the room blowing slightly, as if he had just broken the surface after a deep dive. Meanwhile I had taken on to my knees a sketch-book which had been in danger of shoving my glass off the table, and was idly turning its pages. It was full of pencil studies, none of which had been done yesterday.

In this book there were stray ears and noses and feet and curls sketched about the pages. If they were things of flesh and blood they would puzzle the Salvage Corps of Angels to get them properly reassembled on the Last Day.

It was an old book, I could see, for some of the bits of women he had been modest enough to dress wore the fragments of fashions a quarter of a century old. It dated back to the days when a boy fresh from Montmartre with about fifty pounds of remaining patrimony had come to take London by storm.

London had not been taken by storm. Instead she had let the invader enter by the postern gate, seized him and held him prisoner, neither uncomfortable nor unwilling, given him meat and drink, and allowed him to warm his hands at the fire in the stews.

'Ah,' said Frewland, 'you've got hold of that book at last. I put it there for you. Something I wanted you to see.'

'I thought so,' I said, 'but Hilda Trolland grabbed it first. And then'

'I know, I know! I wouldn't give the cat a kipper's head and leave her alone with that woman. If I did I'd come back and find Hilda nursing the kipper's head, and the cat blaspheming on the top of the bookcase. Seen anything that interests you?'

'Nothing rude as yet,' I answered. 'But then you are always disappointing me.'

'Oh, well, anything that strikes you' His voice trailed away for a moment. 'Have another spot? Oh, I see, you've got one. All right.'

I went on turning the leaves, and presently I held the book towards him.

'Who's she?' I asked, pointing.

He smiled and at the same time jerked up his head to bring his eyes to meet mine.

'That's just the question I hoped you were going to ask,' he said. 'I thought of you directly I dug the old book out. There's a story for you there if you can make anything out of it. Only there's no proper end or explanation, unless you can provide it with one.'

I smiled across at Frewland. 'Do you know,' I said, 'that I've rarely had a plot given me that I can use? And I've been fair game for every feminine pot of poison in the middle fifties who begins, "Ah, if you could only write down the story of my life" '

'I get them,' said Frewland sympathetically. 'They all wish I could have painted them at the time when they were going to be presented—only father lost all his money, so they had to become school teachers instead. Well this isn't a plot. It's just a—well, an incident. There's no end. No explanation unless you can make one. Perhaps it seems worthwhile to me only because it's my own experience. I may as well tell you that that sketch was done at a moonlight sitting, and that I was in bed at the time.

'It was the year after I came back from Paris,' said Frewland, 'and I was three-and-twenty, with a healthy appetite and a capacity for spending money if there'd been any to spend. I'd just come to within exactly tenpence of the end of my tether, and the proprietor of the attic which I called my studio had just sent me a very hinty sort of note about three weeks' rent.

'That particular morning—for I'm thinking of a particular morning—I wandered down High-street, Chelsea, to spend 20 per cent of my capital on a glass of beer. Bitter was twopence a half-pint in those days, and if you told the barmaid that she was like Phyllis Dare she was likely to put one on the slate for you until you came in again.

'Well, I had a sketch-book with me—not that one, but another—and while I drank my half-pint I made a sketch of the girl behind the bar, and afterwards tore it out and handed it to her, telling her how strongly she reminded me of Gladys Whatsemame. But I hadn't got to go any further with that, for in came the landlord, looking like Jupiter after a thick night on Olympus.

'The landlord chuckled like a volcano about to erupt a lava of fat, and in true Olympian manner commanded me to draw him. So I did, and I made it last a long time because he kept having my glass replenished while he posed for me.

'While I was drawing him two or three men came in and looked over my shoulder with that charming courtesy which graces the English middle class. Two chaps wanted to be "done" too, and I charged them a bob a time and polished them off in a couple of minutes each.

And I was just wondering if I should buy myself a decent lunch, or lay in some grub for tomorrow, or have my other shoes mended, when I found Garman at my elbow.

'I didn't know him from Adam then. I hadn't seen him before. I turned and found him looking at me out of a pair of eyes which might have been set in cobwebs, although the rest of his face wasn't old. He was an interesting-looking chap, carelessly dressed in awfully good country clothes. And he'd been through the mill. My God, that fellow had been through the mill!

' "Excuse me," he said in a quiet tired voice. "I see you are a professional."

'I told him that I was, and hoped that the Recording Angel would pass a slight exaggeration or take prophecy in lieu of established fact.

' "You have, if I may say so, an extraordinary knack of catching a likeness. Are you busy?"

'Of course I pricked up my ears and wondered if he was leading up to something, so I made a reply so evasive as to be almost statesmanlike. Eagerness always affects the price.

' "I mean—would you be prepared to accept a small commission?"

' "Well, er" I said. And then to help him out of his difficulty, I said "Er?" again, with a resonant note of interrogation at the end.

' "What will you have?" he said. "Then would you mind bringing it over here and sitting down where we can talk?"

' "Now," he said, "I want you to do a job for me, and I couldn't get any of the big men to do it. They'd turn it down. I know 'em. And you won't find it a bit easy. And I should want you to work down at my place in the country right under my eye—*and not talk* "

'Well, I thought I knew what was coming. A painter can sometimes get pretty queer work offered him by people who ought to have been strangled at birth.

' "If it's anything unpleasant," I told him shortly, "there is nothing doing."

'He read my thought at once and almost smiled.

' "Oh, Lord, man, no! It's just this. I want a portrait of a girl, just head and shoulders. I can describe her to you, show you the exact colour of her hair, show you in other pictures the colour and texture of her skin, do everything but provide you with a model. I can't even show you a photograph."
'He smiled slowly and lit another cigarette.

' "That's why I want you to work right under my eye. It may take you months, of course. In fact, you may never do it. I shall be at your elbow all the time, telling you where you're wrong, telling you when you're getting just a shade nearer to what I want. You'll find it tedious, even heartbreaking. But sooner or later, and by slow degrees, I think you'll get the likeness that I want. Wait a moment before you turn it down.

' "You'll live as my guest, of course, and I think you'll find everything that you want at your disposal. While you're at work and for so long as you care to work—so long as the work may need—I will give you three pounds a week. When it's finished to my satisfaction I will give you five hundred pounds. What do you say?"

'Well, what could I say? I told him frankly that he had set me a task which would have made any of the labours of Hercules seem like a sinecure. Nature has rung countless millions of changes with just a few features and shades of colour. Try to recognise a man or woman by the most minute description possible, and you'll know what I mean. Then—try painting them, without having seen them! I blurted out to him something of this sort.

' "Yes," he said, "I know. But I'd like you to try. I shan't blame you if you fail nor turn on you if and when you want to throw in your hand. Will you come and try?"

'So I went down to the country with him that night, cursing my conscience for turning on me and accusing me all the while.

'He lived in a large manor house in the heart of Sussex, which he had bought during the past dozen years. It was a beautiful place, with wealth and taste proclaiming themselves quietly on every square inch of surface. None of his neighbours ever came near him during the two months that I was there. This was not merely because he belonged to a class which in county society is called Not Quite One of Us—and he wasn't quite—but because he had definitely set himself up as a hermit.

'Years ago he had been crossed in love, but no woman had betrayed him and no man had intervened. Death had been his successful rival. For some reason which I never learned no portrait of the woman he loved survived, or none to which he had access. Thus the poor pathetic devil had sought my help.

'I need not bore you with details of the weeks I spent in that gilded cage. My nerves were screaming like flogged children long before I was through. I'd have chucked it a thousand times and given him back the money I'd saved, but I couldn't bring myself to let him down.

'I was given the gun-room as a studio, and I must have wasted a hundred-weight of paper there. He used to walk up and down behind me, like a lion in a cage, and then come and stand at my shoulder every five minutes to tell me I was wrong. Sometimes I would get the shape of the eyes almost to his satisfaction, but by the time I was getting the nose nearly right he'd find out that he'd been wrong after all about the eyes.

'It went on like that until the night I made the sketch you've got before you now. The job was getting on my nerves—had got on them pretty thoroughly. I found I had an awful job to sleep, and I needed bedside books.

'That night I sat up in bed reading *Roderick Random*, quite jolly and very bawdy stuff. It's in every public library, where they've got the English translations of Ovid's *Ars Armoris* along with Kit Marlowe and Swift at his worst, and ban any amount of modern stuff that is comparatively clean.

'And suddenly, you know—well, I don't quite know how to describe this, I had a queer sensation which wasn't fear or anything like fear. I wish I could make you understand, but there it is. I knew *who* was at the foot of the bed, resting her arms on the rail, her chin on the intertwined fingers of the hands which met just above her breast.

'So I lifted my eyes and saw her—still without fear.

'Oh, there was no doubt at all who she was and why she was there. She had the faint half-smile which I've tried to draw, but it was not for me or for anybody but one man who was not there to see it. And I wasn't afraid and I knew even then that I could draw. Thank God for that!

'In about ten minutes I made that pencil sketch that you've been looking at, and I never made a study more utterly to my satisfaction. And, of course, now I had every detail of colouring by heart. When I had made what I knew would be my last touch I looked up, and the room was empty. But on the high polish of the oak bedrail there were little dark patches beginning to fade, as if warm flesh had rested on them.

'Next morning I pinned the sketch on to a drawing-board in the gun-room, and I was out through one door directly I heard him approach the other. He did not say anything to me when I came back, nor I to him. But I could tell by a faint smear that my drawing had been kissed on the lips.

'That morning I began to paint.

'It took me only three days, and it's the best thing I ever did. Some painters would have scoffed at its reality for cheap artifice, mere camera stuff. But I knew what I wanted to do, and I knew what he wanted.

'When the job was done he just said a "Thank you" which sounded quite perfunctory and got out his cheque book. But when my packed grip was in the hall and the time had come to say good-bye he gave me his hand in a sort of way that I understood.

'It's a long while ago now and I don't know if he's alive or dead. I never heard of his dying, but I hope for his sake that he has passed over, and that God has been kind to him and to her, and given him something better to kiss than a square yard of canvas

'That's all. You're the only man I've ever told and I shouldn't have told you if you hadn't seen something unusual in an ordinary study of a girl's head. So perhaps you were meant to pass along the tale for the sake of others.'

And, of course, you need not believe a word of it unless you like. I've merely done what I suppose must have been my job in telling you.

## By the Looe River

Between Liskeard and Looe, and bounded on one side by the road that passes the well of St Keyne, a ruined house stands in the midst of a ruined garden.

Sun, wind and rain have conspired with the fertile soil to throw such a rampart of thorn bushes around them that the first time Kenniard forced his way through he spoilt a new pair of grey flannel trousers and felt himself smarting all over with little cuts and scratches.

In the garden, however, he stopped cursing and admitted to himself that his pains and trouble had not been profitless. One might tramp the world, he thought, and never see such another picture of beautiful desolation. Little more than the shell of the house remained, and that was so overgrown with ivy that it was only here and there that he caught a glimpse of its red bricks.

Brick houses of any age are rather uncommon in Cornwall, and speculating idly on its history, Kenniard walked through the doorless gap and looked about him.

There was an immediate scurry of rats, and he thought at once that here was undoubtedly the place to bring a terrier if he could borrow one. Then he looked up and saw daylight through the broken ceiling, for little remained of the roof save a few rotten beams. He then made an attempt to mount the stairs, but put his foot through the third one and hastily descended.

Out in the wilderness of a garden he cast about him with his not inartistic eyes. Purple flags grew wild and in great profusion, and red poppies peeped out amongst nettles and bindweed. A ringed snake, astonished at the intrusion, hid itself hastily. In the breeze every flower and weed took unto itself a tiny whispering voice.

Strangely enough, Kenniard was not depressed by this scene of desolation. He even whistled to himself as he trudged knee-deep in waste vegetation and surveyed the house from a dozen different angles.

He was a young man of pleasantly ample means and a taste for vagabondage. For some weeks he had been tramping the Duchy with a sketch-book, and was now staying at Looe. He decided that there was material for a dozen sketches in that wreck of a garden.

So next day he came and began a pencil drawing of a comer of the house; and as he worked slowly and in the interludes of consuming tobacco and pacing up and down it took him three days to finish it. After that he began another, which in turn was almost completed when the need of tobacco goaded him to leave it and walk up into St Keyne.

He was absent about an hour, and when he returned, smoking contentedly, he found an Eve awaiting him in his ruined Eden.

Kenniard stood on top of the bank, behind the path he had trodden through the thorns, and stared at her. She was a tall, slim girl with dark hair, which had become loosened in the breeze. She was hatless and wearing a white silk blouse and a heather-mixture skirt. When he first saw her her back was towards him and she was bending over his sketch.

After a few seconds' hesitation Kenniard removed his pipe and ploughed through the downtrodden brambles; and at the sound of his footfalls she looked round at once. She did not start, nor did she seem embarrassed, and Kenniard noted, not without satisfaction, that she was beautiful. But of the two he was much the less at ease.

'I'm so awfully sorry,' the girl said. 'I had no idea that you would come back and catch me.'

She spoke with a half-humorous air of apology. They both smiled, and Kenniard advanced towards her.

'It isn't finished,' he said, with all the haste of the amateur artist to nip criticism in the bud.

'Oh, I could see that, and I can tell it is going to be nice. I'm glad you don't mind '

Kenniard looked puzzled. He was still rather bewildered at finding this new flower in his garden of thorns.

'For coming in and looking at your sketch,' she explained.

Kenniard's smile broadened.

'I am only too glad to find a merciful critic,' he said. 'But didn't you get rather damaged finding your way in?'

She made a rueful face.

'I'm wearing thin stockings,' she answered, 'and my ankles are a mass of scratches. Still, it was worth it.'

'What, to see my sketch? Thank you.'

The girl laughed freely and pleasantly.

'No, I didn't mean that. This garden is worth coming miles to see.'

Kenniard looked at her with a new interest.

'Do you know,' he said, 'that is just what I felt. And I got scratched and ripped about ever so much more than you did. By the way, as I found it first I feel a sort of proprietary interest in it, but let me say at once that you are very welcome.'

She thanked him with just the least hint of mockery in her manner.

'And do you come here often?' she asked.

'Nearly every day. I walk up from Looe. I say, won't you take a pew. You'll find that camp-stool quite comfortable.'

She sat down at once, and Kenniard's heart warmed to her in admiration. Most other girls, he reflected, would refuse and say they would have to be going; but his instinct, sharpened by experience, told him that she was one of the kind of girls that is called 'nice'.

A spell of silence followed, in which Kenniard vainly speculated on who she was. The breeze had lulled, and there was no sound save the rushing of a little hillside torrent into the narrow stream that is called the Looe River. Kenniard had grown so used to this sound, that, to his ears, it had become part of the stillness. Suddenly she looked up.

'Do you know,' she said, 'this place ought to depress me, and yet it doesn't. It ought to be haunted by something sad, and yet it seems so—so jolly.'

Kenniard, whose thoughts were ebbing towards frivolity, was startled into being serious.

'It's funny you should say that,' he exclaimed. 'That's how I always feel. It's strange it should affect you in the same way, because I'm sure it would look as dismal as death to most people. I've got an impression'

'Go on,' she begged.

'Well, then, I feel that the people who lived in that house years and years ago had an awfully good time, and they've left an atmosphere of happiness behind them.'

She nodded and smiled as if the same thought had also occurred to her.

'The people who lived in that house,' she repeated. 'I wonder who they were.' She turned to his sketch. 'There's another queer thing,' she said. 'You've put in a little yew tree, growing by the porch. There isn't one there, but directly I saw your sketch I thought there *ought* to be.'

Kenniard's eyes grew a little larger.

'I felt there ought to be a yew tree growing there too,' he said. 'That's why I put it in. Two minds with but a single thought—and now I am fined half-a-crown.'

'Why?'

'I always fine myself half-a-crown when I say anything particularly banal. Name any charity you like.'

She laughed absently, and he turned towards the house.

'Just for an experiment,' he said, 'we will see if we can find traces of a tree growing there. '

He walked slowly towards the spot, and she rose hastily and followed him. Together they bent over the earth, and there among a thick tangle of weeds they came upon decayed roots.

Kenniard drew a long breath.

'I don't know if it were a yew,' he said, 'but a small tree certainly grew here once, and the whole business is getting uncanny. What made you come in here in the first place? You had to climb a high bank and wade through those beastly brambles. What made you do it? What made you think it would be worthwhile?' I don't know. I was passing along the road and felt that I wanted to see what was on the other side of the brambles, so I scrambled through. I don't know why I took so much trouble. Then of course I found your sketch and knew that somebody had been here before me.'

'Do you live here?' Kenniard asked.

'No. My people have taken a furnished cottage for the summer about a mile away.'

'Then you know as little about this place as I do. Well, let's stop bothering our heads for a little while and have some tea.'

'Tea?'

'There's a basket containing all materials down there in the stinging-nettles. I'm afraid there's only one cup and saucer, but I can have the saucer. There's an abundance of food.'

He went to the clump of nettles and drew out a neatly-packed basket. Some insects had found their way on to the brown paper covering that shielded the contents, and he brushed them away. The girl looked over the thorn hedge which separated the garden from a long field, richly yellow with buttercups, that sloped down to the stream. And her brows were bent in thought, as of one who vainly tries to remember something.

Kenniard turned out his basket in silence, and shook the little spirit stove to see if it were full enough to boil the kettle. A minute later the stove was flaming amongst the damp weeds. Then he re-lit his pipe and stared at the house as if in search of something.

Presently the girl came over to his side.

'Do you want any bread and butter cut?' she asked. 'I expect I am better at that than you are—more practice, you know.'

'No, thanks.' He pointed down at the contents of the basket. 'They did all that for me at the inn where I am stopping. As you may observe, they think I have a large appetite.'

The kettle boiled and Kenniard made the tea, afterwards handing his companion the teapot and setting down the cup and saucer in front of her. She poured tea into both, and he took the saucer in both hands and balanced it accurately amongst some dock leaves.

As he handed her bread and butter she looked at him, suddenly very serious.

'Do you know,' she said, 'I hate apologizing for my conduct or explaining myself in any way, but really'—she hesitated and a faint blush dawned in her cheeks—'this is the most extraordinary thing I've ever done.'

'Oh, bother conventions,' Kenniard answered, 'surely you're not thinking about *them*'

'As a matter of fact,' she answered, 'I suppose most people would call me very conventional. It isn't that I dislike unconventional people, it's the way I have been brought up and a sort of natural shyness, which I am sure you haven't credited me with. Now you're smiling, but it's true. I can't understand myself this afternoon. I have lived all my life at Wimbledon. But perhaps you don't know what that means?'

'You're not at Wimbledon now,' Kenniard remarked.

'No. But that does not explain why I am willing to talk to a perfect stranger and take tea with him as if I had known him all my life.'

Kenniard looked thoughtfully down at his saucerful of tea.

'Now you've mentioned something else that's very strange,' he said. 'Why do we know each other so well? We do, you know; and we don't even know each other's name.'

'Perhaps it's time we did,' she answered. 'Mine is Joan Hillmer, my father is a solicitor, and I am quite sure you have never heard of either of us.' 'I,' he said, 'am Arnold Kenniard, a restless person much given to wandering, and I am quite certain that my name means nothing to you. You know, Miss Hillmer, there is some mystery here. I hate talking what most people would call drivel, but how comes it that we have the same impressions, the same thoughts about this old ruined house and garden. Think! We both take a lot of trouble to force our way through to a spot that most people would call uninviting. We both find it a happy place when most people would think it utterly depressing. We both think that a yew tree should be growing over there by the porch, and we find that a tree of some kind has been there. You, who are generally so conventional, are not averse from talking to me, and you feel that you know me. I feel that I know you. Now, what does it mean?'

He looked up at her and saw that her cheeks were scarlet. His heart began to beat very quickly and heavily.

'It may mean,' she said, 'that we are both very silly, and—and imagine things.'

He nodded and sipped some tea out of the saucer, feeling a little ridiculous in the act.

'Some people,' he said, 'would talk coldly and scientifically about transmission of thought. But I don't believe that. You had the desire to enter the garden before you met me or dreamed of my existence. Before you saw me you saw my sketch, and knew that I had done right to put in the yew tree by the porch. We both knew that such a tree once grew there. Now how did we know?'

She shook her head. The eyes of both of them were bright with excitement.

'I've travelled over most of the world,' Kenniard went on, 'I've met most kinds of people, but nothing like this has ever happened to me before.'

To himself he admitted that it was vastly pleasant; the very eeriness of it gave him a running thrill of joy. For a long while they sat in silence, thinking, while the afternoon burned on.

Presently Joan arose, and held out the camp-stool towards him.

'Now, please,' she said, 'you are to go on with your sketch.'

'You're not going?' he asked hastily in a tone of alarm.

'No-o.' Her tone was a little doubtful. 'I needn't go just yet. I want to see the sketch finished. It won't take you very long, will it?'

'The trouble is,' said Kenniard, 'we've only one camp-stool.'

'I insist on your taking it. It won't hurt me to stand or sit on the grass. And I want so much to see your sketch when it is done.'

So, reluctantly, he took the only seat, and fell to work again. The girl stood behind him, watching, and they talked for a while. Then she wandered away and into the ruined house, but carne out quickly, and explained with a nervous laugh that the rats had frightened her.

'I'll come in with you,' Kenniard said, getting up. 'By the way—that field down there with all the buttercups.'

'Ah,' said Joan, 'I've been thinking of that.'

Their eyes met, and each looked into eyes that were strangely, inexplicably familiar. A feeling of awe came suddenly upon them both.

'Tell me,' said Kenniard in a low voice, 'what about that field?'

'No,' she said, 'you tell me.'

'I know,' he went on after a little pause, 'that two children have been there—a boy and a girl. And it was a long while ago. Now you go on.'

'I—I can't!'

'Please!'

'It is all so vague. They used to play there. And they were very happy. And the buttercups were—were very' yellow', and seemed to light up the grass as they do today, and—that's all I can remember.'

'Remember!'

'I mean—oh, what am I saying? I don't mean remember. It's all imagination. I've never been here before. You know it's all imagination!'

Her voice rose to the pitch of one who is highly strung, and Kenniard advanced to where she stood and took her by the arm. She did not resent the familiarity, but stood looking up as if lost in bewilderment.

'Come on,' he said, 'let's go and explore the house. I won't let the rats come near you. We can't go upstairs, but we can have the run of the downstairs regions.'

She came with him without demur, and they entered the dusty, damp-smelling ruin of a hall. The rats scampered before them and a hundred cobwebs waved in a perpetual draught. It was very dark inside, for the ivy had overgrown the windows, but a ray of sunlight, coming through the roof and the broken ceiling, made a bright pool upon the floor.

On their left hand a rotten door hung on its rusty hinges. Kenniard set his shoulder against it, and forced a gap wide enough for them to enter the room beyond. There the floor had rotted away in patches, but round by the skirting it still seemed safe, and there he led Joan, walking gingerly. Decay and utter desolation was all around them, and overall was the semi-darkness of a room whose blinds are drawn.

Joan pointed to the far wall with a hand that trembled.

'That's where the picture used to be,' she said.

'The engraving?'

'Yes. You know. The one of Queen Elizabeth on a litter surrounded by her courtiers.'

Kenniard drew a deep breath.

'Do you remember what stood over there?' he whispered.

'Yes'

'Wait! I'll write it down, and then you shall tell me.' He took a notebook and pencil from his breast pocket and scribbled a word. 'Now!'

'A spinet,' Joan whispered without hesitation.

He held the notebook up before her eyes, and in the dim light she saw written the word that she had just spoken. Her breath came with a kind of sob.

'In God's name, what does it mean?'

'You know what it means, Joan,' he said steadily. 'We both know. I don't know this Joan Hillmer who is a solicitor's daughter and lives at Wimbledon, but I know *you*. And you know me—you who lived in this house with me as a child, and played with me in that garden and in that meadow, God knows how many years ago.'

She shrank away from him, and backed a step towards the door. Her eyes had grown larger and her face looked pearly pale in the gloom.

'Oh, what are you saying?' she cried. 'I'm frightened—I don't understand!'

'You do!' Kenniard went on relentlessly. 'Look at me, Joan. What barriers are there between us? You remember what I remember—dim things seen through a haze across the gulf of death and a century of time. You know that we loved and were happy.'

'Oh, don't!'

'You know that we love now, and may be happy again. Look at me, Joan.'

But her gaze was bent downwards, nor did she lift it when she spoke.

'It sounds mad! I don't believe it! Oh, let us go!'

'Listen, Joan.' His voice was hoarse and pleading. 'You know me. You knew me when I stepped into the garden and you could not treat me as a stranger. Now I know why I have spent my life in wandering—searching, always searching after you. Do you think mere chance led us both to the ruin of this house where, in some other life, we used to live? Do you, Joan? And can you look at me and say that you do not love me?'

Still she did not look at him, and now she stood close to the dusty threshold of the door.

'Oh, don't ask me now,' she whispered, it—it is all so strange—so different from Wimbledon, and young men in flannels, and tennis and tea-parties. Be kind to me, and try to understand. Perhaps—another time.'

She lapsed into silence, her face flushing scarlet. And Kenniard, being an understanding man, realized the meaning of her disjointed words. He knew that the soul of Joan Hillmer, which had slept for twenty years in a London suburb, must get used to its new awakening.

He tapped her on the shoulder.

'Come on, then, little Joan,' he said. 'I understand.'

And they passed out in silence into the early evening sunlight.

Standing among the weeds she offered him her hand as if nothing but small talk had ever passed between them.

'I must go now,' she said, in a voice that was hurried and toneless. 'Good-bye.'

He took her hand and strove to look into her eyes.

'You'll come tomorrow?' he asked.

'Perhaps—yes. Yes, I'll come tomorrow. Good-bye.'

'Good-bye, Joan.'

She walked quickly away, passed through the gap which Kenniard had beaten through the thorns, and vanished down the bank. He stood looking in that direction long after she had gone. Then he passed a hand across his forehead and went over to where he had left his camp-stool and sketch-book.

A motor-car sped down the road, leaving a long trail of rising dust, and Kenniard followed it with his eyes.

'My God!' he said to himself. 'The twentieth century!'

Then, as he packed up his camp-stool and the basket of tea-things, a smile brightened his face and a stave of melody came from his lips.

'I shall see her tomorrow,' his heart cried. 'Oh, my love, I shall see her tomorrow. '

## The Lovers

They met that night as usual under the moon, and, hand locked in hand, climbed the steep slope towards the fringe of the woods. It was neither warm nor cold—at least, neither was conscious of temperature. The breeze which caressed without fanning them was a mere stirring of heather-scented air. An atmosphere of peace and languor and content wrapped them around. The moon was a silver lamp hung high in the south. It gave a silver keel to each of the white clouds which sailed above it with the majesty of galleons. He pointed them out to her as they walked.

'They are fairy merchantmen,' he said, 'loaded with toys for little children to play with when they dream—as we are dreaming.'

'They bring kisses from dear dead women to sad old men who smile in their sleep. '

'They bring success to worn-out failures.'

'Some carry a cargo of lost hours for those who live only in the past.'

'I sailed in one of them to meet you.'

'And I in another—to meet you at the Port of Dreams.'

They climbed, as usual, close to the edge of the wood. He felt the ground with his hand before they sat.

'The heather,' he said, 'is warm, like dry sand. Give me your hands.'

She gave them, and he folded them against his knees.

'I love you,' he said simply.

She answered with the same simplicity:

'I know. I can feel that. I know, too, that you can feel my love.'

'Let me drink in your beauty a little while. Your eyes are like pools of dew under the stars. Your hair is a soft mist of gold. Your smile is like April sunlight on a wood of young saplings.'

'And yet,' she said, 'you do not remember.'

'In the strange condition which we call Being Awake?'

'Yes.'

'Nor do you remember me.'

'All love, all beauty is forgotten. We steep ourselves in ugliness. We are greedy for nasty things. We are made so. We cannot help it.'

'Do you remember what you do when you are awake?'

'Not clearly. One has to do foolish things which one pretends to like. It is all very vague. I do not want to remember. '

He laughed softly.

'I have just remembered the name I am known by in that other state. It is Smith. Smith is a foolish name.'

'Can you remember what that part of your life is like?' it is very dim and far off. ... I think I add up figures.'

'To what end?'

'God knows! It is very foolish work.'

She bent over, touching his hands and hers with her brow. Her hair spread about both of them like a soft cloak.

'I wonder,' she whispered, 'do we meet and not know each other?'

'I should know you,' he answered, 'even although I forget.'

'I do not think so. Oh, my love, what does it matter? We have tonight.'

'And many more such, if God is good. Kiss me.'

Their lips met in the shadow of her hair, and while the long kiss lasted they drank love from each other's eyes.

'Your mouth was like a little rose against mine,' he said.

'Lay your hands on my face. Your hands are cool like the leaves of water-lilies.'

'I can see the wood through your hair.... It is very dim and misty.'

'And quiet.'

'I saw a faun peeping out. ... There will be sport in the wood presently. ...Oh, look! Oh, look! ... Ah, they are gone!'

'The drvads?'

'Yes, they crossed the grove. I saw the flash of their white bodies. They are very swift.'

'And shy. Soon'

'Hush! Oh, listen!'

Out of the silence of the wood, thrilling and tremulous, now loud, now dying almost to silence, came the thin, sweet music of pipes fashioned out of reeds. They clung together like children, in awe of the Great Piper, in great fear, and yet in a great ecstasy of sweetness. ...

Somewhere, in another world close at hand, an alarm clock began its shrill stuttering. Mr Harold Smith, bank clerk, sat up in bed with a start and reached out a hand to silence it. Being a very ordinary young man of his condition, he swore aloud because it was already half-past seven.

'I know I've been dreaming again,' he reflected. 'Never can remember what I dream. '

The bedroom was one in a boarding-house near Paddington, and looked like it. In ten thousand other such rooms all over London, ten thousand other young men, all more or less like Mr Harold Smith, were swearing because it was half-past seven, and beginning to drag themselves out of bed. While he dried himself after his bath he sang a very vulgar song which Miss K.N. Pepp was singing just then at the Hippaladium, and hoped that the Chinese breakfast bacon supplied by the boarding-house would be milder today than it was the day before.

In this he was, as usual, disappointed, and at a quarter to nine he set out for the branch of the bank in which he worked. It was situated in Bond Street.

Now it happened that day that he was forced to take his lunch later than usual to suit the convenience of a superior.

And it happened that, as he was returning to the bank at a quarter to three, the Honourable Pamela Lendon was being driven in a great car down Bond Street on a shopping expedition. For a moment, just as he was turning in at the doorway of the bank, their eyes met.

Something in the piquant little oval face set him searching down the labyrinthine roads of his memory. A moment only; then he gave it up.

'Must have seen her driving down this way before,' he reflected. 'Nice little bit of stuff. '

Then he went back to his high stool behind the brass railing and opened a great ledger.

## The Lady of the Chateau

'Come on, there!—keep in touch!'

The voice of a harassed corporal, anxious to get back to the comparative safety of the support trench, rang out sharply on the clear frosty air. The men of the ration party lifted their respective loads—each carried two sandbags full of rations or two petrol cans of water—and began to slip and stagger along the frozen road, past the transport limbers and the little knots of men around them.

The snow had lain for days and its surface was frozen hard. There was no moon, but the air was clear and all around one could see the horizon, a definite line where the white met the black. This virgin whiteness was sullied here and there by fresh shell-holes, and around them the explosive had left dingy stains, like iron-mould on a white cloth which had many holes.

Private Arthur Bainbridge brought up the rear of A Company's ration party. He was small, slim and rather girlish looking despite his camouflage of grime. Officers sometimes stopped him and asked his age. He told them nineteen, which was the truth, although he looked years younger. In civil life he had been a clerk, and he was in the habit of always wearing flannel next his skin and keeping nothing secret from his mother. He had been educated at a small and 'select' academy, where the boys were imbued with spurious gentility which forbade anything so vulgar as fisticuffs.

Despite these disadvantages he was no coward. He had been 'up the line' two or three times before, and he was relieved to find that the stories he had read—the acute agonies of terror supposed to beset a soldier under fire for the first time—were all moonshine, at least with regard to himself. But now the novelty had worn off, and he could feel the appalling misery and dreariness of it all.

He had spent four days and nights in the front line with hardly a wink of sleep. This was the company's first night in support; he yearned, with a longing impossible for anyone but a soldier to realise, for the chance of a few hours' sleep in one of the dug-outs. It meant, at the best, stretching himself on a bed of fence wire with no covering but his clothes, but the prospect came to him like some tantalising dream of Heaven. Once down, the cold and the itching of his skin would not, he knew, delay for a minute the coining of oblivion. There was only one thing in the world worth having, and that was sleep.

'Oh, God, I am tired! Oh, dear God, I'm so tired!' he kept saying to himself; and suddenly wondered if he were saying it aloud.

The sharp stuttering of a German machine-gun broke out in front, slowing, changing its key as it traversed the British line. Bullets hissed venomously about the heads of the party, but the men took no notice. They knew that bullets from that machine-gun always flew high over that spot. As if in answer there came a salvo from our light field guns in the rear, and the sound was like that of giants kicking enormous footballs. One was shrapnel shell, and they saw the flash of it bursting in mid-air nearly two miles in front.

Then the party turned to the right and congested around the entrance to the trench, as one by one the men let themselves down on to the slippery duck-boards.

'Those all the petrol cans you've brought?' inquired a hollow voice from the bottom of Company headquarters dug-out, down which the rations had been passed.

The corporal replied that there were no more.

'Then we're two short. Somebody'll have to go up to the chateau. Detail a man.'

The corporal turned.

'Here, Bainbridge.'

'Yes.'

'Get hold of two empty petrol cans and go and fill them at the chateau. You'll find a well and a bucket on a chain in the cellar. Here's a bit of candle. Got any matches?'

'Yes, but'

'Get a move on, then. The sooner you go the sooner you'll get back.'

Bainbridge tilted his shrapnel helmet back a little from the spot where the rim seemed to be hurting his forehead.

'Can't I have a bit of rest first?' he pleaded. 'I'm so awfully tired, Corporal. I'll go before morning.'

'We're all tired,' said the corporal, 'I'll see you don't do any gas-guard tonight,' he added, not unkindly. 'Better go now while Fritz is quiet. He strafes the chateau pretty often, you know.'

Bainbridge said no more and turned heavily away towards where three or four petrol cans were lying on their sides. The corporal called him back.

'You know the way?' he asked.

I've seen the chateau in the daytime. It's half way up that hill.'

'That's right. Cross the road and follow the trench on the other side—Buckshee Trench it's called—down to the railway. Two or three hundred yards up you'll see a path beaten on the snow. That'll take you straight there.'

Bainbridge thanked him, picked up the petrol cans and went. It was not very far, but he knew how the journey would seem interminable on the way back when the cans were full of water. He knew the chateau well by sight, a battered shell of a house which had in its time endured the onslaughts of British and Germans. The sweepings of a modem battlefield had collected round it as all floating waste in still water finds its way sooner or later to some tree fallen in its midst.

It was strange to think that people had actually lived there less than four years ago—real people, not men half concealed by the mud they carried, scrubby of face, who lived underground and whose wildest hope was that the shell, destined to find them within the radius of its burst, would only maim them. Lovers, perhaps, had walked with linked arms along the terrace, what time there were no vicious gusts of machine-gun bullets to slog the wall behind them. They had come out of a lighted room where there were food and warmth and furniture, and had seen the lights of real trains moving like a string of luminous beads down there in the valley. All this seemed impossible to Bainbridge. He felt somehow that this inferno had always been and must always be.

It was indeed very quiet just then. One of those startling silences, which come sometimes to every part of the front, hung on the air now as dull and heavy as the crust of snow on the ground.

He reached the railway track and began to pick his way carefully from sleeper to sleeper. Once he fell in a small shell-hole and cut his hand on a sharp piece of flint. As he picked himself up, moaning below his breath, he remembered having seen a picture something like it in a high-class English journal devoted to humour. He pictured the comfortable arm-chair people at home laughing at it—without understanding. People who talked—and even wrote—glibly of soldiers laughing in the torments of hell. Pot-bellied wheezing old men who 'only wished they were young enough', and, lying, never realised the depths of their mendacity.

'They'll never know!' he muttered to himself. 'Who can ever tell them? I can't! Nor I nor any man!'

Now he had reached the path leading up to the chateau and turned to the left. He could see quite plainly his destination, the rugged outline of the broken house.  He increased his pace a little.

Phew-ew-ew-zzz—Smash!

The shell, a five-point-nine, dropped midway between him and the chateau. He crouched down, shaken and unnerved by the suddenness of its coming. A fountain of crusted snow, earth and stones went up, and the nose-cap flew singing away into the distance.

'God!' he whispered.

Phe-ew. Phew-ew. Phew-ew. Bang! Smash! Bang!

Five of them this time and all around him. And there was more to come, that was certain. The Germans had started to shell the chateau and the railway-line, and he was caught, void of cover between the two.

More followed and yet more. A heavy piece of metal crashed in a bush beside him and buried itself.

Bainbridge nerved himself to take what he conceived to be his only chance. He must make a dash for the chateau and get into the cellar. He picked himself up and began to run.

Suddenly he slowed down and ceased altogether to hurry. The shelling had ceased as suddenly as it had begun, and with the cessation he became conscious of a change in himself. He was still hungry and ineffably weary, but his body no longer itched and smarted, and he was able to move with less effort than before.

He looked up at the chateau that now loomed close in front of him, and a low ejaculation of surprise escaped his lips. He saw the clean precise outline of a house unscarred by war, white steps gleaming like the snow led up to the main entrance, and, more wonderful still, lights only partly dimmed by their curtains burned in some of the windows. While he stood transfixed by amazement the door opened and a wide bar of light spread itself over the snow. The slim form of a woman stood in the aperture. The figure beckoned to him.

Bainbridge lifted a trembling hand in salute.

'Madame,' he blurted out, suddenly afraid, 'qu 'est-ce que vous voulez?'

'Ah!' cried a voice low and musical, in his own tongue, 'you are English. Come here, little boy! Oh, my poor one, how cold and tired you look. And what a little boy it is!'

Something drew him to the steps and within touching distance of the woman. He knew little of women's dress but he divined that hers was costly; he saw how miraculously it fitted her, and found himself contrasting it with the dresses worn by the women near his suburban home. She was pretty too, and seemed young, or nearly young, and she seemed to exhale an atmosphere of rest and kindness. It seemed to Bainbridge that all tired things must want to come to her and find solace and peace in the shelter of her presence. She might have been an incarnation of motherhood. Suddenly he found that her two little hands were holding his and that she was drawing him gently into the lighted hall.

He yielded slowly, and words came stumbling to his lips.

'Pardon, Madame, I did not know that you were here; I came for water. They told me the house was in ruins.'

Her only answer was a gentle smile.

'But, Madame, you must not stop here. It is dangerous. They send shells here often.' He found himself using that very simple and precise speech in which Englishmen so often address foreigners. The lady drew him over the threshold.

'Come!' she said. 'We will forget the war for a little, you and I. Poor little one, how cold are his hands! You shall rest awhile and have food and drink and warmth.'
In his delight at the mention of the things that were then most precious to him he almost forgot to wonder. He stumbled through the wide hall on the lady's arm, and noticed on his left a bronze figure of a medieval knight in full armour with battle-axe lifted as if in the act of striking a heavy bell that depended before him.

'That,' said the lady, 'was cast by Claus of Innsbruck. It is one of my great treasures.'

Bainbridge had never before heard of Claus of Innsbruck, but the name clove to his memory. He suffered himself to be led into a great salon with a painted ceiling where the light shimmered on gilt and brocaded chairs. The lady led him to a settee before a blazing log fire, and, seating herself, drew him gently down beside her. She herself rose again almost at once.

'You will pardon me a little while, m'sieur,' she said, addressing him formally for the first time. 'I have no servants.'

He smiled feebly. He had hardly known how tired he was until he came to rest on that seductive settee. The lady went, and returned almost at once with food on a tray and something that steamed in a cup.

Bainbridge hardly knew what he ate and drank. He was saturated in comfort now. His hostess watched him as if he were a sick child. His heart went out to her in gratitude.

'Madame,' he said presently, 'if I dared to ask another favour I would beg you to tell me how to thank you.'

She sat beside him again, and, uttering a little cry, seized one of his large dirty hands between her own and pressed it to her bosom.

'Oh, my little one! That you should thank me.'

'I shall never forget,' he murmured.

'I have a son,' she whispered, 'no older than you. Oh! he is big, but he is still my little one, my little boy. He is fighting now—in Lorraine. So it is no wonder, is it, if I love you, my little one?'

He did not resent her way of treating him as a child. He felt strangely like a child again. He began, as a child would, to tell her things about his mother and his home.

She listened with attentive sympathy, and laughed gently, and asked little questions. And while he talked he had an odd feeling that England and home were farther away than ever. Suddenly his eyelids drooped, and the lady, who never removed her gaze from him, uttered a little low cry.

'Oh, you are so tired!' she cried. She passed a slender arm around his shoulders and drew him against her. 'Rest, little one,' she whispered. 'Rest here. '

His head drooped on to her shoulder. The eternal child in every man leaned to the eternal mother in every woman.

'Mother!' he whispered sleepily. 'Mother!'

He gazed into her eyes, and they seemed to widen and widen until they filled all the space between them, and he felt himself being drawn into them. A man's voice from quite near said in English: 'There he is. That's him!' Then Bainbridge fell quietly asleep.

He came to in a base hospital, and swore very, very dreadfully, and fought several orderlies and nurses, for he had just been under an anaesthetic. Then he slept again, and as soon as he stirred in waking became conscious of a voice at his right hand addressing him.

'Hallo, chum! How yer feelin'?'

Bainbridge smiled wanly, and turning beheld part of the face of a very jovial gentleman whose head was picturesquely swathed in bandages. 'Not so bad, thanks,' Bainbridge murmured. 'What's the matter with me?' 'They've taken a lump of shell casin' out of your 'ead, and you've 'ad a big toe knocked orf, and a few odd bits of stuff in your left arm. You're lucky, considerin' you 'ad a whizz-bang all to yourself. You'll be able to swing it with that missin' toe and get your ticket. I've 'ad four packets, but I can't get nothin' worth havin' like that.' And the patient in the next bed stretched himself and sighed.

'Shall I get to Blighty?' Bainbridge asked.

'Ra-ther! As soon as you're well enough to be shifted. I say, do you know a bloke in your crowd named Sadler?'

'Yes.'

'He's here, in another ward. He was one of the party that came to look for you. Got his packet—a cushy one in the leg—while they was carrying you back. We come down in the Red Cross train together, and he told me all about you. You got yours outside the old chateau, didn't you?'

'Outside the chateau?' Bainbridge repeated in a troubled voice.

'Yes. You'd gone there for water, 'adn't you, and walked into a strafe.'

'I thought,' Bainbridge began. Then, suddenly, he shut his lips and relapsed into silence.

'Funny thing,' said the much-bandaged gentleman; 'I know that chateau well. I was there in 'fourteen, when Fritz was havin' it all his own way. Shan't forget that place in a hurry, neither, nor the lady wot lived there.'

'The lady!'

'Yes, a real lady too. She wasn't half good to us chaps. Just like a mother she were. Used to make coffee for us and cook grub, and wouldn't charge nothing. Do it all herself, she did, her servants having run away. She wouldn't go, even when they begun to shell, though our officers was always beggin' her to. She said her son was a soldier an' she was goin' to stand by the soldiers.'

Bainbridge stared blankly at his ward-mate.

'What—what happened to her?' he asked faintly.

The other felt for a brand-new hospital handkerchief, and blew his nose violently.

'She copped out, poor lady!' he said. 'One of the best she was too. She wouldn't go, and Fritz went for that chateau soon as he got 'is guns up. He knocked the place to pieces one night, and we found her under the dee-briss in the mornin'.'

He waited as if for some comment which was not forthcoming. Then he resumed:

'Some of 'er furniture and pictures an' things was worth 'undreds and 'undreds of quid, I've heard tell. Our officers wanted to get some of it out before Fritz came, but there wasn't time. I remember a statue she 'ad in the hall—a bloke in armour takin' a swipe at a bell. That was worth a pot of money. My officer told me the name of the bloke wot done it, but I forget now.'

Bainbridge found his voice.

'Claus of Innsbruck!' he cried.

The man on his right lifted himself a little in bed, and leaned across.

'Now, 'ow,' he demanded in a tone of deep wonder— 'ow in the 'ell did you know that?'

He leaned farther over, stared at Bainbridge, then whistled and turned away.

'Orderly!' he cried. 'Orderly! Or-der-lee! Come 'ere, you blinkin' base-wallah. I want some note-paper quick—an' the bloke in the nex' bed 'as gone an' fainted, or something!'

## In the Waters Under the Earth

Mr Besley kept pace with old Sadler, watching his movements with amused interest. There was nothing mysterious or awe-inspiring in the appearance or the actions of this shaggy-whiskered old yokel who had spent three-quarters of an average lifetime in cutting hedges, clearing ditches, and making himself generally useful in field and copse.

But he had the gift which no scientist denies and none seeks to explain. Mr Besley, who had been dragged to consult clairvoyants and fortune-tellers during an irritating phase through which the late Mrs Besley had passed, could not help thinking that if old Sadler and others who practiced his peculiar art paid a little more attention to what he would have called 'the trimmings', water diviners might inspire that reverence which savage tribes bestow upon their witch-doctors.

Mr Besley was known almost to have retired from business in London, and he was now walking on the plot of ground on which a new bungalow was destined to appear, and in which he intended living after his complete retirement.

The plot of land was a mile outside a residential Sussex village in which a number of other retired business men had made their homes.

Having bought the ground and approved the plans which an architect had drawn more or less in accordance with his desires, the question of water supply naturally arose. The spot was too far from the nearest main for connection to be practicable or even possible, therefore it was necessary to sink a well.

Mr Besley had heard of water-diviners, but like so many other dwellers in the great cities he did not believe in them. He thought that water-divining was a country superstition, like believing in witchcraft, ghosts and pixies.

But when he heard that everybody else in that locality had had the source of his water supply 'divined' for him, he became mildly interested. And when the estate agent's assistant assured him that 'divining' water was cheaper, surer, and in every way more satisfactory than the most up-to-date and scientific methods, Mr Besley was entirely converted.

The estate agent's assistant was a very modern young man who said 'Quite' in answer to nearly every question, parted his hair in the middle and wore an article of jewellery which is generally described in advertisements as a gent's gold Albert.

If he could speak of water-divining in the same casual tone that he would have applied to motoring or the kinematograph there could be nothing very mysterious or superstitious about it after all.

Old Sadler didn't pretend that there was. He said that it was something that some could do and others couldn't, and that he was one of those who could, and that he was bothered if he knew why.

If he walked slowly it was for obvious reasons, and not as part of a ritual He carried in his two hands, between the finger and thumb of each, a forked twig freshly cut from a hazel bush. It was pliant and not so thick as a lead pencil, shaped like a catapult of which the handle had been cut off within an inch or two of the forks.

He carried it by the two forks waist-high and parallel with the ground. Mr Besley waited, watched, and in due time saw the phenomenon occur.

The hazel fork miraculously became alive. It twitched, writhed, and then began to bend. Mr Besley instinctively watched old Sadler's hands and held him innocent of trickery. Except that it was bending upwards and downwards, the hazel twig was behaving just like the top joint of a fishing-rod under the play of a fish.

'Here we are, sir,' said old Sadler without emotion.

'Well, I'm blessed!' exclaimed Mr Besley. 'You're sure there's water under here?'

'Sure,' returned the old man thoughtfully. 'But I don't know as I should sink a well just here.'

'Why not? Too deep?'

'No, I don't reckon as it'll be what you call deep. But this ole twig keeps pullin' to the left, and I ain't never known un do that afore. '

'What does that mean?' Mr Besley asked anxiously. 'Bad water?'

'No; 'twould be good spring water sure enough. But I've never known ole twig do such a thing afore. There's plenty water hereabouts. I'll find another spring in a minute. '

'I wonder whether that twig will twist about for me if I stand in the same place. May I try?'

Old Sadler surrendered the humble instrument of divination.

'Like enough, sir,' he said. 'Lots can do it but don't know until they try.' Mr Besley tried, but in vain.

'Now,' said his companion, 'you stay still, sir, and let me put my hands on your shoulders.'

Instantly Mr Besley felt the fork writhe between his fingers, and he dropped it promptly. Previously he had said that he was blest; what he said now amounted to precisely the opposite, and he used a much stronger expression.

'I don't like it!' he exclaimed, and uttered a shamefaced laugh.

Old Sadler misunderstood him.

'I dunno why ole twig wanted to pull to left as he come up,' he said shaking his head. 'I've never knowed un do that afore. I shouldn't sink no well 'ere, sir.'

Mr Besley looked around him. With the imaginary bungalow in view, old Sadler could have divined water at no more convenient place.

'Well, if you say the water will be all right, and probably not too deep down, I don't see the objection. In fact, this is just where I shall want a well.' Old Sadler volunteered no more advice.

'Very good, sir,' he said. 'Best mark the spot then.'

Mr Besley had taken lunch at an inn about half a mile distant and had arranged to return there for tea. Old Sadler's way lay in the same direction and the two walked together. Mr Besley fell into easy conversation.

'Do you know,' he said, 'that I am acquainted with hundreds of people who wouldn't believe it possible to do what you've just done; and when I tell them I've seen it done they won't believe me.'

'Very likely,' answered old Sadler, trudging stolidly beside him. 'I've met some o' they.'

'And you don't in the least know what makes the hazel fork wriggle about and point upwards?'

'I dessay it's got something to do with that there electricity.'

'I can't see how there can be any electrical affinity between a twig of hazel, the human body, and water thirty or forty feet underground.'

'Well, there it is, sir. Some can do it and most can't. Sometimes the gift comes from father to son, and sometimes it misses. My old father could do it.

'And there's some says as they can do it with metal, though I never tried, so I can't say how true it is. The twig rises for water and dips for metal, they say.

'But I can't think why ole twig wanted to lean over to the left as he come up.'

'Well, I don't understand the whole business,' said the puzzled Mr Besley from London.

'There's nobody as does,' muttered old Sadler. 'I reckon 'twas a gift given by Providence, so as people a long way off rivers, as would have died without water, could always find it.

' 'Twasn't necessary as many should have the gift, and only a few 'ad it, as only a few 'ave got it today. That's all we're meant to know, and that's why nobody can't tell us no more.'

'A good many funny things happens from time to time that nobody can't explain, because we're not meant to understand 'em.'

As these were observations with which Mr Besley, being a reasonable man, could not possibly quarrel, conversation then languished; and a few minutes later, having reached the inn, he paid the water-diviner the small sum demanded and took leave of him.

Two or three weeks later the well was sunk. The two men at work struck water at thirty-five feet, and finished their job, brickwork and all, in less than eight days.

The other men who were employed in building the bungalow were paid by the hour and did not work with this passionate zeal. Mr Besley came down to see how they were getting on, and he was not pleased.

What also displeased him was some news he learned at the inn—to the effect that a human bone had been found by the men who had been sinking the well.

They had taken it to Dr Hardelot, who pronounced it to be a human shin-bone, but longer and thicker than the average, and in his opinion a relic of prehistoric man. The depth at which it was found precluded any other supposition.

Now Mr Besley had no particular use for the shin-bone of a prehistoric man, but he was a great stickler for his rights. For all he knew to the contrary the relic might be of value, and, since it was found on his property, surely it was his bone!

What, then, had this Dr Hardelot done with it, and what right had he to do anything with it at all?

It happened that the man who had been at work down in the well at the time entered the bar shortly after Mr Besley heard the news, and the landlord sent for him to come and be interrogated.

'Yes, sir,' he said, 'that bone come up in one of the last buckets o' dirt before I struck water. In fact, I found water just as my mate on top shouted down to say what had just come up in the bucket.

'There's no doubt the whole skeleton's there, but I hadn't the time to grub it out. The spring was a strong one, and the water comin' in fast, so I had to make haste and brick up.

'Any'ow, the rest of 'im can't be got out now, for there's brickwork round him and five-and-twenty foot o' water on top. Not that I see it matters, for it seems he must be one o' them pre'istoric coves—a prime evil man the doctor called him—wot doesn't need decent Christian burial.'

'Ah, yes, you took the bone and showed it to the doctor. Very natural, I'm sure. And what did he do with it?'

'I can't say what he did with it, sir. He gave me five bob and said as it was very interesting, and what a pity the other bones couldn't be recovered. He said as it must have belonged to a prime evil man, thousands and thousands of years old.

'And he said as the depth I found it at went to show how the surface of the earth must have risen since them days, all through the dust and dead leaves settlin' in layers. That's what he said, sir.'

This still did not explain why Dr Hardelot had appropriated the bone, and Mr Besley was determined to see him.

'And,' continued the digger of wells, 'I'm not sorry as I hadn't time to look round for the rest of that bloke. That job give me the 'orrors, or rather the end of it did.

'I'd just laid the last brick, the water was bubblin' up fast, and I'd stepped into the bucket and given my mate the signal to draw me up, when something like a pair of arms come out of the water and collared me round the legs.

'My mate at the top couldn't turn the windlass and called down to me to ask what had got stuck. I couldn't answer because I was just paralysed.

'Then some'ow I kicked myself free and felt myself bein' drawn up. But it gave me a rare turn, I give yer my word, sir. '

Mr Besley stared incredulously.

'Something like a pair of arms!' he exclaimed. 'Did you *see* them?'

'No, sir, but I felt them all right. Great thick arms they was, and as hard as iron. I couldn't possibly see nothin' for, bein' about to come up, I'd put out my light and—I don't know if you've ever been to the bottom of a well, sir? No? Well, it's about the darkest place ever.

'You can look up, and you see a bit of sky no bigger than the nail of your little finger. If the sun's shinin' the sky looks no brighter than moonlight, and often you can see a star or two in broad day.

'No, I didn't see nothin', and perhaps it was just as well. I wouldn't go through it again, not for anything. Don't ask me wot it was got 'old of me, because I don't know.'

Mr Besley suspected that the man was drawing on his imagination in the hope of extracting a tip, but he did not like to say so.

'And another thing 'appened after that,' continued the victim of the experience, 'which put the wind up me. You can ask my mate about it if you like, for he seen the same thing.

'The first bucket o' water that we drew up out o' that well looked just like blood for a few seconds. Yes, sir, just like raw blood straight from the slaughterhouse.

'My mate and me, we just stared at it and gasped, and then, in a flick of the eye, we saw that it was only water after all—and very good spring water at that. But it was a bit funny, wasn't it, sir?'

Mr Besley did not think so at all. He reflected that he would soon be compelled to use the water from that well for drinking purposes.

Then it occurred to him that the man was very likely poking quiet fun at him to see how he would take it, and he came to the conclusion that his most dignified course was to laugh as if he appreciated the joke, and tip the fellow half-a-crown. This he did, and the digger of wells sidled away to drink it.

It happened that there was more than one small cloud in Mr Besley's sky at that time. He had decided to spend his declining years in the most peaceful and secluded district he could find within a short radius of London; and having definitely committed himself, he found that the district had ceased to be peaceful and secluded.

A few days before, there had been a most appalling murder in a village some five miles distant. A little girl who had been sent out at night to call in the local doctor to attend her mother had literally been torn to pieces, as if by some ferocious animal.

There were rumours of a wild beast having escaped from a private menagerie, although all the practical amateurs of zoology in the south of England denied having lost one.

Still, rumours were current of a bear or a great ape—the descriptions did not precisely tally—being seen at night in the district in which Mr Besley proposed to make his home.

Another annoyance, from Mr Besley's point of view, was the slow progress which the builder's men were making with his bungalow. The contractor had been apologetic and had assured Mr Besley that he, himself, would be out of pocket over the business.

Something was wrong with the men. They were slow' over their work because they were obviously afraid of something. Doubtless it was through these rumours of a wild beast having been seen in the neighbourhood.

All this was very bad for the temper of a London business man who was known in his small circle of acquaintances and employees for one who stood no nonsense. All that he asked for now' was a measure of peace, for the wheels of his existence to revolve on well-oiled hubs. So far was he from
that ideal that the eyes of the world had been focused close upon the place of his intended retirement by the committal of a ghastly murder, and by a popular belief that some escaped wild beast had taken up its quarters there.

Added to which there was that disturbing, although doubtless mendacious, story about the well. And, to crown all, some miserable country general practitioner had stolen his prehistoric bone! Horace, returning from a visit to Maecenas to find his Sabine farm the scene of unorthodox plebeian revels, could have been no more annoyed.

Mr Besley stayed the night at the inn and called on Dr Hardelot next morning. The doctor he found to be a youngish man with an ascetic face and sprightly manner, a combination producing a personality difficult to overawe.

Dr Hardelot at first supposed, or pretended to suppose, that Mr Besley had called to see him about the bone from motives of sheer academic interest.

'My dear sir,' he said with enthusiasm, 'it's a glorious discovery—glorious. The crying pity is that it is now next to impossible to recover the whole skeleton. I should guess that the man to whom it belonged was between seven and eight feet tall and as strong as a gorilla.

'I am not an expert, and I can't say to what age the owner of that bone belonged or, to within a few thousand years, when he lived. Taking the depth at which it was found into consideration I should say that the bone can't be less than six thousand years old

'Older than the Piltdown remains, I should think. By far the most interesting discovery that has ever come my way!'

Mr Besley said something to the purport of what he had meant to say, but by no means as he had meant to say it. The doctor listened with an air of apology accompanied by a belying smile.

'Oh, I see! So it was found on your property? I'm awfully sorry, but how was I to know? Workmen bring me tilings they find, and I just bung 'em into the local museum After all, it's the proper place for 'em. One doesn't decorate one's wife's boudoir with the shin-bones of one's prehistoric ancestors.

'It's now in the museum at Carsham. But I'll tell you what I'll do—I'll drop 'em a line to say that it was found on your property and that they've got to thank you and not me for presenting it.'

After all, what could one do with a man like that? Mr Besley removed his foot from the near-side stirrup of the high horse which he had vainly attempted to mount.

'Of course,' he agreed weakly, 'the museum's the proper place for it. What sort of man was he, do you think—the owner of that bone? To look at, I mean.'

Dr Hardelot shook his head.

'I'm not an authority,' he answered, 'and I couldn't even guess what period he belonged to. Probably he was much bigger than the average man of today, but not so good looking. Much more animal, you know, and not much brains in his low, flat forehead.

'Hairy all over, I should think, and strong as an ox through leading a natural life Went out and caught his dinner when he wanted one, and ate it raw. Couldn't speak intelligibly, but gibbered like a big ape. That's how I picture him. I may be wrong, of course.'

Mr Besley constructed for himself this not very pleasant picture.

'Had he a soul, do you think?' he asked suddenly and surprisingly.

Dr Hardelot smiled.

'I don't know what a soul is,' he said, 'and I doubt very much whether any of us possesses such a thing. If he had, it must have been stupid and ferocious and abominably cruel.

'It's just as well his type has vanished and—to quote the schoolboy howler—"nothing remains of the dead except their bones".'

But Mr Besley was not so sure of this. For no particular reason, but for a variety of small and apparently detached causes, which his mind was busy trying *not* to assemble, he rather doubted it.

Those who lived in that part of the country, and most students of sensational journalism, will remember the wild animal scare in north Sussex two or three years ago, and the extraordinary number of cases of sheep-worrying and injuries to cattle. To the same cause was also attributed the violent death of the small girl.

Quite a number of people alleged that they had seen the escaped beast, and not a few swore that they had been chased by it However, descriptions of the monster varied considerably.

Some were sure that it was a bear, and others were equally certain that it was a gorilla. It was huge and brown and hairy, and walked upright, and, strangely enough, it was only seen at night.

Naturally, these stories threw the countryside into a panic, and, among the many inconveniences suffered by individuals, the progress of Mr Besley's bungalow was still further interfered with.

Men cannot work when they are forever looking over their shoulders, and, by a piece of bad fortune, Mr Besley's plot of land seemed to mark the very centre of the disturbances.

After a while Mr Besley came down to stay at the inn, and spent his days walking around the skeleton of his future home, and, by trying to keep the men at work, acting as a sort of unofficial foreman.

It happened that one evening, after dining at the inn, Mr Besley felt for his cigarette case and felt in vain. It was a presentation one, and gold at that. After a moment he realised where he must have left it. He had taken it out and laid it down on the window-sill of one of the rooms in the bungalow, just as he and the workmen were about to leave.

In order to make reasonably sure of recovering it, he must walk up to the bungalow alone and in the dark, an action which very few people in that neighbourhood would have been willing to perform just at that time.

Mr Besley had courage of a sort, and he also had a fussy little mind which hated to lose even small things of no intrinsic value. These two qualities now combined to lead him forth to face the terrors of the night.

It was not very dark. There was no moon, but the skies were clear and the stars burning brightly. He reached the bungalow unmolested in something less than ten minutes, crossed the doorless threshold, and laid his hand down unerringly on the cigarette case.

As he emerged he opened the case, took out a cigarette and fumbled for matches. The acts of striking and lighting brought him to a halt in the waste of mud which was some day to become his front garden.

What a fine night it was! Fairly light, and the air so clear. No; not quite so clear after all. There was a little mist, rising over yonder. Queer-looking mist, too.

Blackish stuff instead of white and—Good Lord, yes!—it was coming out of the mouth of the well, oozing out with a pasty suggestion of oiliness, and rising to a height of between seven and eight feet!

Mr Besley watched it fascinated and unafraid for the first few moments. After that he watched it, still fascinated, but very much afraid. It was taking a definite shape, becoming solid, becoming neither man nor beast but a hideous combination of both.

It was brown and naked, hirsute and clumsy, and as it turned a great cumbrous head in the direction of Mr Besley he caught a dull glow of angry, bestial eyes, and a white gleam of protruding fangs.

Mr Besley uttered a loud cry, threw up his hands and fled. It was almost a fatal movement, for it drew upon himself the unwelcome attention of the man-beast. Mr Besley was elderly and in no condition for running, and the chase lasted barely thirty yards.

When he felt its breath on his neck Mr Besley threw himself flat and lay still. Somewhere there lurked in his tortured brain a memory of having once heard that men pursued by bears had escaped by shamming death. Once on the ground, he did not move, simply because he did not dare to.

Flat, heavy feet shambled around him, and he heard a grunting and gibbering. Then a wheezing noise sounded a little nearer and he realised that the Thing was getting on to its knees beside him to give him closer examination.

A great hand set with long, sharp talons rested on his sparse hair and then began to stroke it. It was just then that Mr Besley fainted.

When consciousness returned to him he was alone, and later he found himself back at the inn with no clear memory of how he had managed to get there.

The disturbances ceased shortly afterwards as suddenly as they had begun. At about that time a mild local sensation was caused by the theft of a bone from the Carsham Museum.

The museum was not often visited, and it was comparatively easy for anyone to break open a glass case in broad daylight and abstract the contents—although why anybody should wish to steal an old bone the museum committee was at a loss to guess.

The identity of the thief was never discovered, although some have made a shrewd guess; for it is on record that Mr Besley threw something into his new well before causing it to be bricked up and cemented. On the following day the services of old Sadler were again requisitioned.

'Ah!' said he to Mr Besley, as they walked together over the plot of ground, 'I don't know why you 'ad t'ole well bricked up, but I knew some'ow as you wouldn't find un satisfactory.

'Never knew ole hazel twig to pull to the left afore. Ah! here we are, sir. More water here. '

Mr Besley looked, fascinated. The fork of hazel was rising, apparently of its own volition, and the short end was pointing at the sky.

'All right this time?' Mr Besley asked anxiously.

'Yes, sir,' said old Sadler, reassuringly. 'See the ole twig pointin' straight up? Everything all right this time.'


**Wine of Summer**

'This is really my cousin Frank's story,' Mrs Bamby announced to the group sitting in the gloaming by the open French window looking on to the garden. 'He wrote an account of it which I have here, and which I think I had better read to you. I don't know that he tells it particularly well, but I should probably tell it worse if I relied on my memory. I am very much inclined, when I try to tell a story, to begin in the middle and end at the beginning. Frank Cayley has never tried to publish this story, because the preparatory school of which he writes is still in existence, and quite a flourishing concern. It would be impossible to recognise the school from his description, particularly as he has taken care to alter every name, but the facts are known already to a few, and public curiosity might enlarge the circle of those who know them, and do harm to the man whom Frank calls "Mr Tappington."

'I think I must trouble you for one candle, so that I can see to read. Perhaps by the time I have done some of you may be glad of it.'

When the candle had been fetched and lit, she unfolded the manuscript and began to read.

I was round about thirteen when this strange and dreadful thing happened. It was the year Cicero won the Derby, and if I had by me one of those sporting calendars, I could soon tell my exact age at the time. At any rate, I was still at my private school, and working hard for a scholarship to Rugby—which I never got.

For obvious reasons I cannot mention the school by name nor describe at all accurately where it was situated. It was, however, at a South Coast town where there were many preparatory schools, so that we had full fixture lists at football, hockey, and cricket. Our school was a big, modern house, with a shrubbery in front, around which a wide drive performed a semi-circle; and from the upper windows you could see over the shrubbery and across a road, beyond which was a sandy beach, which marked the farthest territory of the sea.

I suppose ours was like hundreds of other such schools, although I shall always regard it as the best. It prepared boys for the public schools and the Navy, coddled them with home-comforts, saw them through childish ailments both mental and physical, and allied itself with the parents in teaching decency and manliness, and good sportsmanship. We hear a great deal of the public school tradition, and so little of the spadework done first by such men as old Tappington.

There were about fifty of us all told, in my day, ranging in ages between six and fourteen. Tappington, then quite young, was an ideal schoolmaster. He had been a county Rugby footballer, and was an old Cambridge boxing blue. His sister, a funny, severe little woman, with a sense of humour, had taken a nurse's diploma so as to know exactly what to do when a boy coughed or fell down when roller-skating. And he had gathered around him half a dozen young assistant masters, who were really first-class fellows. He treated them like brothers, and ourselves like sons, so no wonder we were like one big happy family! Parents growled over the bills they received—it was not a cheap school—but they got good money's worth.

Tappington's methods were considered rather unusual in those days, although they're more the rule than the exception now. He understood the boy mind and treated us as individuals. If innocence prompted some unfortunate child to ask an embarrassing question he did not lose patience, but answered it as frankly and truthfully as possible. He joked with us like our own fathers and uncles, and often read us stories during working-hours when he thought our application deserved some such respite. He never caned a boy without saying something kind to him after the punishment, and urging him not to be a silly young ass in future. We could always talk to him frankly and, up to a point, familiarly, and treat him as a friend.

It so happened that on an afternoon in May, there was a minute or two to spare between the setting of preparation and the time for dismissal. Tappington had been taking the top Form, of which I was a member, in geometry; and while we packed up our books and waited for the bell, he fell into easy conversation with us.

'What's going to win the Derby this year, sir?' asked a boy named Burrows.

'Cicero,' said Tappington without any hesitation.

He was correct, but it was not a remarkable feat of prevision. The horse was a hot favourite all through, and started at odds-on. Somebody groaned, and Tappington laughed.

'Backed something else and lost a fortune, have you, Irons?' he chaffed. 'Some of you don't like Cicero, I know.'

This was an allusion to the fact that some of the classical high lights were reading *'In Verrem, Actio Prima.'* Irons bubbled at the mouth in acknowledgment of the joke.

'Oh, sir, he's beastly. I don't think a horse with a name like that ought to be allowed to win the Derby. What about Jardy, the French horse, sir?'

'He's coughing, my poor Irons, if that's your fancy. You had better invest your pocket-money on Cicero—only don't let me catch you.'

The whole class laughed comfortably. Cicero, as a hot favourite, was not worth any schoolboy's shilling. Of course, practically no betting went on among the children, but some of us bigger ones—the would-be bloods—invested tiny sums on the Derby. The butler, whom for some unfathomable reason we called Pompey, was so obliging as to act as bookmaker's agent in such transactions. I don't know if Tappington knew what went on. Probably he did, and deemed it expedient to turn a blind eye on it, so that we might lose our money and learn a salutary lesson early in life.

We none of us liked to ask if he knew of a possible outsider—it would have been too barefaced—so I shifted the topic a little by asking if he were going to his Derby Day dinner that year. There was in the town a certain retired colonel, an old owner and breeder of racehorses, who always celebrated the day by giving a dinner in the evening to which Tappington and his staff were invited. Only one master remained on duty, with the result that discipline in the dormitories was a great deal relaxed. Tappington looked at me, and a network of jolly wrinkles grew around his eyes.

'If I celebrate Derby Day with a feast, Cayley,' he said, 'it's no reason why you should. If I hear of any crumbs being found in Number Two Dormitory this year, I shall make searching inquiries. Now go along—there's that bell at last. '

We all filed out, laughing. Tappington had got us beautifully about Number Two Dormitory, but not until then were we aware that he knew what had happened last year. There was very little that that remarkable man seemed not to know.

Before tea there was an interval of ten minutes, giving us time to put away our books in Big School-room and for problematical ablutions. I walked to my desk in the company of Desmond O'Rorke, a diminutive, sad-faced Irish boy, whose propentialities for devilment were belied by great melancholy grey eyes and an air of dreaming pathos.

'I've just had a ten bob postal order,' he announced. 'Cicero isn't worth backing, so I'm going to have a shilling on something at a hundred to one.'

'What's the good of that if Cicero's going to win?' I demanded.

'Cicero won't win just because Tappy thinks it will. I don't suppose it'll win at all. I think I shall make myself dream the winner.'

'How do you do that?' I wanted to know.

'I don't know how I do it, but I did it once. There's a racecourse near our place at home, and we had a house-party once, and a man named Sir Humphrey O'Flynn was staying with us, who owned one of the horses called Lass o' Limerick. He told us all the night before that it couldn't win and that he wasn't going to back it, and was only running it to get it used to a lot of people and noise. Well, that night I dreamed that it *had* won, and I told him so in the morning. But it took me an hour before I could persuade him to back it.'

'And of course it won?' said I, with a gentle note of sarcasm.

'Oh, yes, it won all right, at twenty to one. And the O'Flynn man had five pounds on it, which he said was only a nibble. But he bought me a bicycle and a stamp album, and told me if I had any more dreams like that I was to be sure and let him know.'

'Well, don't you dream about a loser,' said I, 'or you'll be jolly well rooted. '

'If I dream about one he'll win,' said young O'Rorke very seriously. 'I *am* like that, you know. I saw my grandfather once. '

'So did I—last hols.'

'But mine died before I was born. It was his ghost, you know. I'm the sort that sees ghosts. They all say so in my family.'

Most of us regarded young O'Rorke as being more entertaining than truthful, and I gave him a look which drew from him an indignant protest.

'But it's *true*. And we've got a banshee in our family—'

'Oh, try a sardine with it!' I interrupted, this being our fashionable catch-phrase at the time for putting a period upon a profitless conversation.

Still, I spread the story, and, although O'Rorke was laughed at, there was not a few of us who were waiting to stake an odd shilling on any horse which he might dream about. But time wore on, and the young Joseph failed to oblige. Meanwhile, such respectable and supposed-to-be innocuous daily papers as were placed in the library to allow us to see the cricket news informed us that Cicero was growing a more and more raging favourite.

Two days before the race we told O'Rorke that he could dream what he liked, for our financial interest in the race was killed by the disappearance of Pompey. Pompey was a soft-living, full-bodied man who, we alleged, drank Tappington's best port out of a bucket, and who certainly could not afford to take liberties with his constitution. That year the warm weather had tempted him into the sea a month earlier than usual, and he paid the penalty with a chill; and he went off to recover in the house of his sister, who kept a lodging-house on Marine Parade. Our line of communication with the local bookmaker being thus cut off, we reconciled ourselves to the thought of saving our pocket-money and merely taking an academic interest in the race.

And that very night O'Rorke announced to an audience consisting of the occupants of Number Two Dormitory that he knew the winner.

'It's got a funny name,' he said. 'It's called Wine of Summer.'

None of us had ever heard of it, and we said so.

'Nor had I until just now,' said O'Rorke.

'When did you dream that one?' Burrows asked. 'If you fell asleep during chapel, you young pagan hog, no good will come of it.'

'I didn't dream it—so go and suck tin-tacks. I had it told me.'

'Who by?' was the general and ungrammatical query.

'By the new Pompey, if you want to know.'

'The new Pompey!'

We were all immediately interested.

'I suppose he's a sort of a kind of a substitute until Pompey himself recovers from the shock of taking a bath.'

'But what's he like, and where did you find him?' I asked.

'He's awfully like a butler,' said O'Rorke, with laboured sarcasm, 'and I found him in the boot-room.'

'Then he can't be like a butler if you found him in the boot-room. Old Pompey wouldn't deign to put his nose in there.'

The boot-room was a small and windowless apartment leading out of the day-room—or, rather, such windows as it once possessed had been covered over by the numbered pigeon-holes in which we kept our boots. When the house was a private residence, we understood, the day-room had been the dining-room and the boot-room a butler's pantry. The boot-room was dark even in the daytime and a gas-jet—convenient for roasting chestnuts in the season—was always kept burning.

'Well, I suppose the new Pompey had lost his way. Anyhow, just before chapel I remembered I'd blanco-ed my cricket boots and left them out in the sun and hadn't remembered to bring them in. So I went and got them and took them into the boot-room. Some silly ass had blown out the gas, and inside it was about as black as Burrows' finger-nails—Shut up, Burrows! Pax! No, it wasn't as black as that—as them—because I could see a chap sitting on the bench, and he was wearing a shirt-front and looked like a butler, so I guessed what he was.

'I said, "Hallo! Are you the new Pompey?" And he answered in a very solemn, deep voice, "I am the butler"—just like that. So then I asked him what was going to win the Derby, and he got quite excited and said "Wine of Summer."

'I wasn't going to tell *him* I hadn't heard of it, so I said I didn't think much of it, and asked him if I thought it could beat old Kickero. Then he got still more excited. "He *will* win," he said. "He *must* win!" '

'Fat lot he knows about it, I expect,' remarked a boy named Lindsay.

'I don't know,' said O'Rorke defensively, 'I dare say he's just come out of service in a big house. Servants do get jolly good tips sometimes. Their masters and their masters' friends tell them things. And this Wine of Summer must be a hundred to one shot. It gave a list in the paper this morning, and said a hundred to one the others.'

There was a moment's spellbound silence.

'A hundred shillings is five pounds,' announced an awed voice.

'A hundred times two shillings is ten pounds,' said somebody else, 'and I want a bicycle with one of those new three-speed gears.'

'How are we going to get it on?' asked Burrows.

'Oh,' said I promptly, 'the new Pompey'll see to that. He seems to know the ropes. What sort of chap is he?'

O'Rorke was struggling into his pyjamas.

'Oh, I don't know. I could hardly see him. He seemed tall and thin, and he had a very white face, and he looked horribly worried. I wasn't talking to him more than half a minute. The bell had already gone for chapel and I'd been late already twice this week.'

A voice came up the staircase: 'No talking there!'—and conversation was not resumed until the lights were out, when we whispered for a while before falling asleep. I confess that I lost consciousness while trying to multiply three-and-ninepence—my entire worldly wealth—by one hundred, and subtracting the tip which the new butler might lawfully expect.

We saw no new butler on the following morning, and there was a rush of us to the library before lunch to see if the papers had anything to say about Wine of Summer. They had not. There were a few horses headed by Cicero and followed by Jardy with quotations against them, and the list concluded with 100—1 others (0). We were innocent, and we saw nothing ominous in the length of odds which was presumably to be obtained against the new butler's fancy. If we had seen Wine of Summer quoted at twenty-fives we should have been disappointed. As it was, we went in to lunch and looked out for the new butler.

Again we were disappointed. A maid waited at the master's table, and Mr Vallance did the carving. The staff seemed to be short-handed, but the world seemed to go on very much as usual without our Pompey.

Later in the day Burrows achieved an interview with Annie, one of the dormitory maids, and asked about the new temporary butler. Annie denied knowledge of any such person, and moreover professed herself ignorant of the method and means of putting money on a horse. She had sixpence in a sweepstake, she said, through the medium of a friend of hers in a local laundry, but her interest in the Sport of Kings began and ended there.

Books were hurled at O'Rorke in the class-room that afternoon, while we awaited the belated coming of the young man whose duty was to teach French; and first pillows, then gym shoes, and then boots assailed O'Rorke in the dormitory that night. O'Rorke retaliated with spirit. My 'Pendlebury' lost its cover and Leader major's pillow went through an open dormitory window on to the front drive. O'Rorke fought the world and stiffly maintained that there *was* a deputy butler—who might have been found wanting and sacked at very short notice—and that the said deputy butler had tipped him a horse called Wine of Summer.

The following day was Derby Day. Since it was obviously impossible for us bigger boys to put our shillings on a horse we began to concentrate more than ever on our Derby night supper. Dormitory Two had always been celebrated for its Derby night supper, and this, I fear, was less in honour of the occasion than because we knew that 'Tappy' and all the staff except one would be dining out. You mustn't misjudge us. We debated among ourselves as to whether it was quite sporting to take advantage of such an occasion, but decided that Tappington had plainly told us that he knew what went on, and had given us a bland hint either not to be caught or to expect unpleasant consequences.

The school shop, run on a co-operative system by the head boy, provided most of the essentials. A maid, who had the afternoon off, smuggled in loaves of bread out of the public fund, and executed one or two private commissions. Many shillings which the obliging Pompey would otherwise have handed over to the local bookie were distributed in a better cause. A doughnut in the dormitory when you are thirteen is worth ten dinners at the Ritz when you are thirty.

We got an evening paper through Annie, who was interested in the laundry sweepstake. Cicero won at odds on, Jardy was second, and I forget the third. Wine of Summer didn't run, and a disposition further to chastise O'Rorke was mitigated only by the fact that in no event should we have put our shillings on Cicero.

Our *recherche* meal was to begin as soon as we felt that our unwonted quiet has lulled Miss Tappington, and the one master who had been left behind, into a sense of false security. We dispensed with hors-d'oeuvres and soup, but our fish course was long and varied, and consisted of specimens carefully preserved in tins. O'Rorke felt under his pillow and then uttered a soft and polite curse.

'I left two tins of lobster in the boot-room,' he explained. 'Meant to nip round and get 'em after chapel, but forgot. Wasn't going to take 'em into chapel in case the Tappington woman noticed my pockets bulging. Who'd like to run and get 'em?'

No one volunteered to go, so eventually O'Rorke went himself, and we sat waiting for him to come back. We waited, and waited, but still he didn't come. Then it occurred to us that he must have been caught and that we were likely to receive a visit from Authority, so we made haste to remove all traces of the intended repast. Still nothing happened, and at last Burrows and I crept downstairs on a scouting expedition.

We made straight for the boot-room, which we knew to have been O'Rorke's objective. There was just enough light to see by, for a tiny jet of gas was burning blue. And there was O'Rorke lying face downwards and quite still on the floor.

I made sure that he was dead, but when we turned him over he began to shudder and moan, and when he grew to a completer consciousness he sobbed and clung to us and begged us to take him away.

It took some minutes to get him upstairs, and on the way he gasped out the cause of his trouble. In the boot-room, it seemed, he had seen once more the man whom he had imagined to be the new butler, sitting in the same place as before, and the man had shown him a ghastly white face of despair and had drawn a razor across his throat.

It was useless our telling him that there was no sign of such a man while we were in the room, and that it must have been his imagination, and when I suggested fetching Miss Tappington he clung to my arm in a kind of frenzy and exclaimed:

'No, no, don't tell them! Don't tell them! I couldn't bear telling *them!*'

Well, we got him into bed, but as he continued to sob and moan we got scared again and I went and fetched the matron. O'Rorke was hauled off to the infirmary, and that was the last we saw of him. We next heard that he was suffering from a breakdown and that his parents had come and taken him away. He never returned to the school.

Now the queerest part of this story, I think, is the sequel.

It was about a month later, and we were playing Dunley House School at cricket on our own ground. I had gone in first, and been caught at the wicket off the first ball of the match. In the circumstance I was not feeling too bright, and as soon as I had got my pads off I went and lay down in the shade of a hedge and tried to solace myself with chocolate. After a bit Colonel Trueland—he who had given the Derby night dinner—came ambling around the ground. He took a great interest in cricket and used to attend most of our matches. He stopped when he saw me.

'Well, W.G.,' he said, 'how did you get on?'

I told him sheepishly, and after a word or two of cheerful condolence he would have passed on, but a thought leaped into my head and I detained him with a question.

'Excuse me, sir, but would you tell me if there's a horse called Wine of Summer?'

'Young man,' he said, staring hard at me, 'who told you to ask me that?'

'Nobody, sir. We were having an argument among ourselves. Some said there was a horse called that, and some said there wasn't.'

He continued to look hard at me and at last, it seemed, acquitted me of having tried to pull his leg.

'There *was* such a horse,' he said. 'I owned him, and I wish now that I'd never seen him. I thought he was going to win the Derby twenty years ago.'

Twenty years ago!

'I'll tell you a little story about that,' he continued. 'It may teach you not to gamble when you grow old enough to be tempted. I was very confident about Wine of Summer's chance. I put more money on him than I could afford, and I told all my friends.

'Your school was a private house in those days, and Sir Francis Fastnidge lived there. Sir Francis told his butler about Wine of Summer, and the poor silly fellow put all his savings on to the horse and borrowed more money besides. And a ghastly thing happened as a result. On the night of Derby Day when the news about the race had become known, the poor wretch committed suicide in his pantry. He cut his throat with a razor.'


## The Caricature

Five guests had already assembled at Lilton Gate when Vair arrived to make the sixth. In her letter of invitation Francesca Hughes had hinted at some of the delights of the 'cottage' purchased by her husband after a series of fortunate speculations. The shooting had not been looked after for years, but there were plenty of partridges. There was golf within walking distance and over a mile of salmon fishing in the Lyddy. There was some cubbing to be had, and the Ulchester September race-meeting would be held before the party broke up.

The occasion was of the nature of a house warming; 'but not a crowd,' wrote Mrs Hughes, 'only just two or three people we really want to have.' Eileen Baxter, she added, was to be one of them.

Eileen Baxter was the lure which attracted Vair to Lilton Gate. He had seen her a great many times during the past few months, but not often enough. As a bachelor to whom many doors were open he had used all his ingenuity and tact to place himself under the same roof as Eileen. Sometimes he was successful, but generally she was elusive as a shadow. Francesca Hughes, therefore, earned and deserved his blessing.

He arrived in the afternoon and, having failed to announce the time of his train, traversed the two miles between the station and the house in an ancient fly. The 'cottage' which stood on a little wooded knoll overlooking a broad coil of the Lyddy, disclosed itself as a country mansion of considerable size.

Little of the brickwork could be seen for creepers, but Vair's hazy knowledge of architecture told him that the house was not very old—sixty or seventy years at the most.

Vair did not recognise the servant who admitted him. He had expected a greeting from Toombs, who had 'buttled' for Johnny Hughes's father

'What have you done with old Toombs?' he inquired as he handed over his hat and stick. 'You haven't mislaid him somewhere, I hope?'

'He's had an accident, sir,' said the man. 'Fell downstairs the night before last.'

'Really! I'm sorry. Pretty serious for a man of his age and weight Not badly hurt, I hope?'

'Nothing very serious, sir. Only a few bruises and a shaking. He had a day in bed yesterday but he's up again today, and he'll be at work tomorrow.

Would you like to go to your room, sir?'

'Thank you. Mr or Mrs Hughes in?'

'Mrs Hughes and the ladies are out but expected back to tea. The gentlemen are in the billiard-room.'

'All right. I'll get you to show me the way there directly I have had a wash.'

The billiard-room he could see at a glance had been added by Johnny Hughes. It was a long room built out of one side of the house, with a skylight and two rows of windows. His appearance interrupted a game of snooker-pool between his host and two other men of his acquaintance. Johnny Hughes, a hearty, red-faced man of forty, having made him welcome, laughingly suggested that the game should now finish, as his was the lowest score. Leslie Stroud, who was leading, at once became clamorous with feigned indignation. General Clariette, the third member of the party, took advantage of the interruption to help himself to another whisky.

'Oh, please carry on,' Vair said. 'I'd like to watch, and there are only three more balls to go down. Who's the lucky man who's on that blue?'

'Me,' said the old general, picking up his cue; 'but I don't fancy it much. It might double, perhaps ... Hi, young man! Don't you sit on that chair!'

Vair had been about to plant himself in a chair near the fireplace. He started at the warning voice and turned to stare at the chair behind him. It was ordinary enough in appearance, of dark wood, with a leather cushion accurately fitting the seat.

'Why not?' he asked. 'What's the matter with it?'

'What's the matter with it?' Johnny Hughes repeated. He rested his cue in the angle of a pocket and passed around a comer of the table. 'I'll show you what's the matter with it. I must have that chair returned to the lumber-room or somebody will be hurting himself.'

He lifted a foot and placed it on the seat of the chair. As he exerted pressure the legs of the chair spreadeagled until the seat touched the floor. Then, as he removed his foot, the chair sprang up again. There were springs, concealed in the angle of the legs and seat. It was the sort of trick chair that one sometimes sees in a knock-about turn on the variety stage.

'That's rather useful,' Vair remarked. 'How did you come by that?'

'Found it,' said Hughes. 'It was among a lot of lumber in one of the attics when I bought the house. I had the shock of my life when I sat on it. It collapsed under me, and then, when J picked myself up, there was the chair standing up behind me as good as gold.' He laughed reminiscently, and added: 'I had it brought down here to show Stroud.'

Vair sat in a chair guaranteed by his host to be safe.

'Now who on earth,' he said, 'could have wanted a thing like that? Who was the late owner of the house?'

'Don't know anything about the last people who lived here. The place had been on the market for several years. Funny taste in furniture they must have had ... Oh, bad luck, General!'

'I hear old Toombs has had an accident,' said Vair, lighting a cigarette.

Hughes paused in the act of taking a shot.

'Yes—poor old chap. Of course, you haven't had time yet to find out that we're bewitched. You'll know it though before you've been here very long.'

'Bewitched!'

'In the middle-ages we should be out looking for the blood of a cross-eyed woman. Ever since we've been here there's been—oh, good shot!—there's been a series of annoying little accidents. Nothing very serious, mind you. Poor old Toombs's fall is by far the worst of the lot. But things have been broken in the most mysterious way, and we've been cutting ourselves shaving and losing our studs and tripping over things in the dark for all the world as if some malevolent fate had got its knife into us.'

'Somebody cuts the buttons off my shirts every night,' remarked the general. 'I'll swear somebody does!'

The game came to an end with Stroud fluking the black. The men put up their cues and gathered around Vair.

'The pink ball disappeared this morning,' Stroud remarked. 'We found it under a bush in the garden. I low it got there, Heaven knows. '

'Poor old Toombs,' said Hughes, 'swore blind that somebody jumped on his back and whistled in his ear when he fell downstairs. He still sticks to it.'

Vair rolled his gaze in the direction of Leslie Stroud.

'Ought to be more careful, Leslie,' he observed.

'Fortunately,' said Stroud, 'I have an alibi. We were all in the dining-room when we heard the crash.'

'I ought to mention,' said Hughes feelingly, 'that he fell down the whole flight of the kitchen stairs with about half our best dinner service. '

'It seems to me,' Vair said laughing, 'that you're being worried by a poltergeist'

'I don't know what a poltergeist is,' Stroud remarked, 'but it's an odds-on certainty that you'll be troubled by it, too.'

'Nothing German about *us*,' Hughes said, echoing the laughter of the others.

'A poltergeist,' said Vair, 'is a mischievous ghost, generally that of a little boy. He heaves coal about the place, and breaks china and trips people up.'

'We must have got a young family of them here,' said Johnny Hughes.

They all laughed. It was still a joke to them—a series of irritating coincidences.

On the following morning Vair inveigled Eileen Baxter into a round of golf, and they drove up to the links in a two-seater borrowed from Johnny Hughes.

They went once round and then, having the course to themselves, sat on the lip of a bunker close to the last green.

'You've come on a bit since I took you on last,' Vair remarked. 'Playing much?'

'A bit. I was above my form this morning, and that's funny, because every time I drove off I expected the club to break in my hand.'

He smiled. 'Apropos of the long string of accidents?'

'Yes, you've been singularly fortunate so far. Nothing's happened to you.'

'Except that I seem to have tom my dress trousers across the knee. I can't think how I could have done it. Johnny Hughes' man pointed it out to me this morning when he came in to collect my clothes and brush them. Oh, that reminds me.'

'Of what?'

'Do you ever suffer from waking dreams?'

'What are they exactly?'

'Well, just when you open your eyes sometimes you see an odd kind of face looking at you, and you stare, and you find it's a piece of furniture, or the fold of a curtain, which has taken on that look for the moment. I had one of them this morning first thing. I saw a living caricature.'

He thought she was staring at him strangely, and smiled.

'I don't know how else to describe it,' he said, it was exactly like an exaggerated caricature of somebody in one of the papers. It had a grotesque, enormous head, hardly anybody, long legs, and enormous feet. It had a huge mouth, set in an inane grin, showing enormous teeth. Its expression was ill-natured, without being exactly wicked. It looked vacant, inane.'

He was conscious that Eileen was staring at him scarcely breathing, her eyes wide and a little dilated. He smiled to himself because she was taking it all so seriously. After all it was only a dream.

'And,' she added, in a queer strained voice, 'it had ass's ears.'

It was his turn now to stare.

'Now how on earth did you know that!' he demanded. 'You're quite right—it had.'

'I saw the same thing, too,' she said in a muffled voice. 'You've described it perfectly.' She was looking away from him and fidgeting with her hands. 'I woke up and saw it in my room the night before last—the first night I came down. '

'Do you have waking dreams, too?' he stammered.

'I suppose I must. I sat up in bed and rubbed my eyes, and then the thing seemed to melt into the window curtains.'

'Mine resolved itself into my dressing gown hanging over the end of the bed. It's funny we should both have the same sort of dream.'

'Very funny,' she agreed, still looking away from him.

'Two minds,' said Vair, 'with but'

'Oh, don't! Was it a dream?'

'What else?'

'I don't know … I don't like the house. I've been afraid.'

'Oh, that's absurd. I don't believe in ghosts. We were all attributing our little accidents yesterday to the work of a poltergeist, but we weren't serious. After all, if there is any sympathy between us, Eileen, why shouldn't we have the same sort of dreams? And talking of there being a sympathy between 'Let's talk about luncheon,' she interposed hastily. 'We shall be late if we don't go back at once.'

She rose up and stood on top of the bunker. He had no option but to pick up his bag of clubs and rise, too.

'In future,' he said lightly, 'I shall be able to blackmail you. I shall eat heavy late suppers, and get the most awful nightmares. Then if we both dream alike, you'll have the same dreams.'

To his surprise she slipped her little hand inside his arm, and spoke almost tremulously.

'Don't tell the others about it,' she begged, 'and please don't let us discuss it any more. If it was a dream, I don't want to dream it again And if it wasn't'

'Oh, of course it was,' Vair said with a laugh. 'I jolly well know that mine was. The thing I saw simply couldn't have existed outside of an illustrated paper.'

'There was a murder in the house once,' the girl remarked, going off apparently at a tangent.

'No there wasn't, Mademoiselle Morbid. Somebody was accidentally shot years ago. That's what Johnny heard anyhow, but he doesn't seem to know any of the details. He was telling us about it in the dining-room last night after you people had cleared out. Now for goodness' sake let's talk about something cheerful.'

The butler, Toombs, almost recovered from the effects of his accident, was on duty again today, and waiting on the small luncheon party. It was immediately after the meal there happened another of those inexplicable accidents which had lately been vexing the household.

As the men filed out of the dining-room into the hall, Vair heard his feet splashing in water, and saw a slow stream flowing lethargically over the polished boards on which his feet were resting. Hughes uttered a mild oath, and pointed to the door next to the dining-room—that of the butler's pantry—from beneath which the water was pouring. In an instant he had flung open the door and rushed inside. Water was pouring in a slow cascade from the flap of a dresser within.

He removed a tray full of glasses from the flap, lifted it up, and disclosed a small leaden sink brimming over with water, and two taps both of which were turned full on. A rubber plug on a chain was fixed firmly over the waste pipe.

Hughes removed the plug and turned off the taps. The sink emptied itself in a couple of minutes.

'Damn! damn! damn!' said Hughes. 'Where's that fool, Toombs? In another ten minutes we should have been flooded out. '

He returned to the dining-room, and kept his thumb viciously pressed against an electric bell until Toombs appeared.

'You saw that ghastly mess in the hall?' he demanded.

'Yes, sir. What's been the matter?'

'The matter? You ought to know that. If you turn the taps on in the butler's pantry, and go away and forget all about them, you must expect a certain amount of moisture to escape and get about the house.'

'I beg your pardon, sir.' Toombs was dignified and slightly resentful. 'I haven't used the pantry sink today.'

'Oh. don't talk rubbish.'

'I beg your pardon, sir, again. I only use the pantry sink for glasses, and such things that I pay particular attention to myself. I did all the glasses late last night, sir. The plate always is, and always has been, washed-up downstairs. Why, sir, the flap's been down over the sink all this morning, and there was a tray of glasses standing on top of it, waiting until I had time to give them a proper polish.'

'I know there was,' said Johnny Hughes. 'I had to move the tray to turn off the taps.'

Toombs had the invaluable gift of being able to point out facts and prove himself in the right without seeming to triumph.

'Well, sir,' he said, 'I don't know how to account for it. As you moved the tray yourself, sir, you'll understand. I haven't touched that tray since eleven o'clock.'

Hughes was simmering down. Toombs was an old servant and faithful man, and he was plainly as mystified as anybody else.

'Then who could have done it?' he asked. 'Who's been in the pantry?'

'Nobody but myself until just before luncheon, sir, as far as I know. None of the other servants ever go there without I tell them to.'

Hughes dismissed him with a nod.

'All right, Toombs. Not your fault, I'm sure. But it's damned queer.'

In that he had the concurrence of everybody present.

Vair slept fitfully that night; his brain had taken on one of those fits of activity which make complete rest impossible. First of all it was Eileen Baxter who filled his thoughts, then other and less pleasant subjects possessed his mind.

Eileen had said that she did not like the house, and now, as he lay there in the dark, he came to realise that he, too, did not like it. Strange that she should have had the same dream as himself—that bizarre, inhuman figure, which had melted away under his waking gaze. With the darkness now taking strange shapes before his eyes he echoed her query—Was it a dream? Now that the thought had been put into his head he seemed aware of a strange presence in the house—a presence which, if not entirely sinister, was not of this earth. And how else to account for the strange succession of stupid and ill-natured jokes which had been perpetrated?

Of the three men guests he could rule out himself. The old General, pompous and dignified, was the last man in the world to commit such misdemeanour. Leslie Stroud was quite incapable of making such a requital of hospitality. Besides, Stroud himself, in going to bed, had tripped over a ewer in the dark, evidently placed in his doorway for that purpose, and had been all over the bachelors' wing looking for the blood of the practical humorist.

The women could also be ruled out. Women do not do such things.

Besides Mrs Hughes, there were only Eileen and her mother and an old spinster friend of their hostess. As to the servants, they were all well treated and satisfied and there was no mischievous boy on the staff. No, the affair was a mystery, and not the sort of mystery that he enjoyed cudgelling his brains over in the dark.

Somehow, it all seemed to him to connect in some way with that collapsible chair found in the lumber-room. How, he could not say. There was a missing link somewhere ...

Then, while he turned the matter over in his mind, he fell into a fitful doze, to be awakened with a start by a commotion at his bedside. He sat up with a cry to find the room lit up, and the General, purple and fuming, standing over him in a mustard-coloured dressing-gown.

'Damn you, sir!' fumed the old soldier. 'Have you been fooling about in my room, wearing a mask and throwing my clothes about?'

'Damn *you*, sir,' cried Vair, forgetting himself for the moment. 'Can't you see you've just woken me up?'

'Then who's been doing it? I woke up, hearing some of my clothes being thrown up to the ceiling. I was hardly awake when my own dress trousers sailed straight into my face. When I looked again there was a huge damn-fool face grinning at me. I don't know what became of the fool; the room was pitch dark. Come and look at it.'

'Well, it wasn't me, and I'll swear it wasn't Stroud. Somebody must have come into the wing. '

'They can't! They can't!' the General cried. 'I took the precaution tonight of slipping the brass catch across the baize door and shutting us all in. The catch is still up; you can see it from outside. '

Footfalls sounded outside the door and Leslie Stroud appeared in his pyjamas, frowning and muttering.

'What's the trouble?' he demanded.

They could see that his sleeping-suit was wet through. 'I fell over the other infernal ewer,' he explained. 'It was put there for me on purpose, when I got out of bed. You people woke me up. What the deuce is the matter? I'd like to know who's playing these idiotic jokes.'

'Whoever it is,' said the General practically, 'he's shut up here in the wing with us. I slipped the brass catch over the door. The only thing to do is to search every room.'

They searched every room, but the landing of that wing, entirely self-contained, concealed nobody. The floor of Leslie Stroud's room was flooded. The contents of the General's trunk and suit-case were flung all over his apartment. And no culprit was to be found.

After half-an-hour, and not without some mutual suspicions, the trio retired to their respective rooms, and once more Vair dropped off into a fitful slumber.

Once more he was awakened—this time by a scream from the landing.

He jumped out of bed, slipped his arms into a dressing-gown, opened the baize door, and ran out on to the great landing, where a female figure rushed to him and flung itself into his arms. It was Eileen, her hair streaming, her eyes wide with terror. Clinging to him she broke into a paroxysm of sobs.

'I've seen it! I've seen it!' was all she seemed able to say at first.

He petted the forlorn figure in his arms until presently she looked up and began to speak coherently between sobs.

'I—I heard something moving in my room, and woke up. And there it was, standing beside the bed, grinning at me ... the—the Caricature. I rubbed my eyes but this time it—it didn't go. It seemed to know how frightened I was and to be enjoying it. I screamed and ran out—I didn't know where I was going. And—and I think it followed me. I knew, the first time, that it wasn't a dream. I wouldn't have stopped here another moment if it hadn't been for you. '

Not knowing what she was saying she spoke the simple truth that was in her heart Even in the horror of that moment he felt his pulses leap at the knowledge that, after all, he was something to her. He bent and kissed her cold forehead and cheeks and called her foolish baby names. So easy to kiss now, when they, human beings clinging together, seemed to be encompassed by forces not of their world.

'I should catch the first train in the morning if it were not for you,' he whispered. 'Don't be afraid, dear. I think you know I love you, don't you, Eileen? I won't let anything hurt you. Now you must go to your mother's room and spend the rest of the night with her. And don't be afraid. I am going to dress and sit on that chesterfield, and keep watch. I shall hear you if you call.'

Half-an-hour before luncheon on the following day Johnny Hughes shepherded his men guests into the billiard-room whither Toombs brought cigarettes and *aperitifs*.

'Of course,' he said, 'you all want to go, and I don't blame you.

Francesca and I are off, too, after what I've heard this morning. I can't tell you how sorry I am for what's happened, but I think you'll have to acquit me of knowing anything about it.

There's no reason why we shouldn't all foregather here next month. I understand that these disturbances only happen in September. I've been to see the local vicar this morning and he told me all he knew about the house. I've read ghost stories and talked to spiritualists, and until the last few hours I thought the whole thing was flam. Now—well, what can any man think?'

'What did the Vicar have to say?' Vair inquired.

'He told me that over twenty years ago the house was in the hands of a silly young fool with a mania for practical jokes. He was never happy unless he was playing them. He had all sorts of mechanical devices for startling people and making them uncomfortable. That collapsible chair I found up in the lumber-room must have been one of them. No sensible man minds an occasional practical joke so long as it's harmless. But this fellow played too many and went too far. His career ended in a tragedy.

'One September, I understand, he had a few men down here for the shooting, and carefully paved the way for what he had in mind by telling them that the house was haunted. There's generally one nervous man who involuntarily gives himself away. There was in this instance, and he took a revolver to bed with him. Then, when his host appeared at his bedside draped in a sheet, the poor fellow screamed and shot him dead.

'Some other people had the house shortly afterwards, and they complained of the same things happening as have been annoying us, and seeing some grotesque thing in the distorted shape of a man But the disturbances only happened in September, round about the anniversary of the tragedy. I suppose the Vicar's theory is the only one—that just as the fellow behaved in life so he is compelled to behave afterwards. '

There was a long spell of silence. Only the heavy breathing of the four men was audible. Then Vair, stretching out a shaking hand for a glass, said:

'But—but why does he take that grotesque shape?'

'I don't know,' said Johnny Hughes, it may be that when a man crosses over, his looks change in accordance with the life he has lived, while he keeps some slight semblance of his earthly appearance. After all, if that is so, what should such a man look like but a caricature of his former self—a huge head, a vacant grin, ass's ears? I don't know, and none of us know. Next month, thank God, we can come back. '

Vair got up and turned his back on the others while he pretended to examine an engraving on the wall.

'I hope,' he said in a muffled voice, 'the poor thing will find peace at last, for its own sake. Somehow, I believe I owe it something.'

## Miss Jessica

'I didn't believe in ghosts,' said Frensworth, 'until I bought Wychfold. '

He had sat silent for a long time, listening to a discussion, half-serious and half-frivolous, such as is generally to be heard when such a subject is broached among people of varying opinions. Now he broke into the debate, and in such a tone as to turn everybody's gaze in his direction. He had a very quiet, expressive voice, and he spoke with an air of having settled the whole vexed question. It was rather amusing to see six or seven people, all more or less fond of the sound of their own tongues, waiting eagerly and in vain for him to continue. For he needed prompting.

'And after you'd bought Wychfold I suppose you still didn't believe in them?' somebody laughingly suggested after a while.

'No, I was converted. I was converted in the only way possible to a man of my temperament —by the evidence of my senses.'

'Is Wychfold haunted?' I asked. 'I used to know it years ago, and it never looked like a haunted house to me. '

'It's not the house,' said Frensworth, 'it's the garden.'

'So you keep your ghost in the garden?' laughed Mrs Orme. 'How convenient to be able to do that. But how uncomfortable for the poor ghost. It must be a man. You wouldn't be so ungallant as to treat a lady ghost like that.'

'It is a lady,' said Frensworth, with a faint smile.

'And you've actually seen her yourself?'

'Oh, several times. We all have.'

'And aren't you afraid?'

'Well, yes, in a certain way. And she seems to know that and avoids us as much as we avoid her. Actually she's a very charming woman—or spirit—and there's nothing at all to be frightened of. I've never known her deliberately to scare anybody but once. And there was a good reason for that.'

'But what was she like? And are you sure she was a real ghost, and not somebody dressed up? And who was she supposed to have been in life? And have you ever tried to lay her?'

We fired our questions at him one upon another, and he laughed gravely and held up a hand in protest.

'One question at a time, please,' he begged. 'Or shall I answer them all by telling you everything, I warn you, you won't believe me. Without the experiences I have had I could never have credited such a story. But two of you men have promised to come down and shoot next week, and you may see something of her. But it isn't a good time. It's in the spring and summer when the gardens are looking their best that we see Miss Jessica most often. For she was passionately fond of her flowers, and that, I think, is why she is to be seen in the gardens and not in the house. '

Of course we clamoured for the story. Here it is. It is impossible, of course, for me to re-tell it exactly in Frensworth's own words, but I shall do as best my memory will let me. At least, I shall put in nothing of my own nor leave out anything important of his.

I bought Wychfold just after the War. The property had been on the market a long time, but it had been by no means neglected. We found the house quite fit for us to move into; and the gardens were in really admirable order, with a staff of men ready and waiting for a new master. You would have said that the property was the apple of somebody's eye, and that money had been lavished to keep it perfect; as indeed was the case. The place had belonged to a maiden lady, the last of a family called Sidderley, who had left directions in her will as to its upkeep while it remained in the hands of the trustee. Before actually coming to live at Wychfold I heard a great deal about this Miss Sidderley, who had been born in my home, and died there, too, with a gulf of sixty years between. Everybody called her Miss Jessica— Jessica being her Christian name—and in the village her memory was loved and revered as the memory of a saint. She was one of those rare women against whom, it seems, none has a word to say. She ruled the village despotically; her word was law against which there was no appeal; but it was a kindly despotism, and the cottagers were as pampered a lot as you would find in any of the shires. Even the drunkards, the wife-beaters, the rustic Lotharios who came under the lash of her tongue—for she was not all milk and sugar—loved and respected their Miss Jessica, and there are a thousand stories told of her kindness to the sick and sorrowing and needy.

She had been beautiful as a young woman, and we learned that age had robbed her of nothing save the gold on her head, for the gold turned to silver in early middle life. We were told that at sixty, when she died, she had the face and figure of a young girl, and a delicate transparent skin which many a young girl might have envied.

I don't know why she never married. Perhaps she was too fine and fragile; perhaps passion had never touched her, and she preferred her roses and carnations to men, for she loved her garden, and her flowers were like children to her.

We heard all about Miss Jessica, but not until we were actually living in Wychfold did we learn that among her old tenants and servants she still lived as something more vital than a beloved memory.

I was going around one morning with Hudson, the head gardener. Nobody could have complained of the condition of things out of doors, but I had in mind certain alterations to suit the taste and convenience of all of us. Among them was the removal of a flower-bed and the extension of a lawn to make a third tennis court. Hudson looked a little troubled and began to scratch the back of his head.

'Well, sir,' he said, 'I don't say as it couldn't be done. But I don't know as Miss Jessica would like it.'

I am afraid I made some jesting reply. One likes, of course, to respect the wishes of the dead, but one can do that sort of thing ad absurdum.

'I don't think we'll let that stand in our way,' I added, 'as Miss Jessica won't know anything about it.'

'Oh, won't she!' exclaimed Hudson, with a rather startling vivacity. 'And if she doesn't like it she'll soon let you know it, too!'

I stared hard at the fellow.

'I don't think we understand each other,' I said. 'I thought you were speaking of the Miss Jessica who is dead.'

'So she is, sir, in one manner o' speaking. But in another manner o' speaking she isn't. She still comes round the garden about twilight-time, having a look round, like she used.'

The man was so matter-of-fact that he fairly took my breath away. Then I looked at him closely to see if he were trying a joke on his new master.

'Do you mean her ghost?' I demanded.

'I dunno what else you'd call it, sir.'

I was surprised and secretly amused. Naturally, I didn't believe a word of it, but the fellow was so very much in earnest that I hadn't the heart to laugh at him. So I asked all the questions that you've been asking me.

'Oh, we've all seen her, sir!' he said. 'You can ask Joe King or Harry Dean or any of the outdoor men!'

'I think you've all seen something at a distance which looks like'

'Oh, no, sir!' he interrupted. 'We've seen her close, too. It was Miss Jessica. There couldn't be anybody else in the world exactly like her.'

'Does she speak to you?' Automatically I found myself asking questions.

'No, sir, she just looks.'

'It's the most amazing statement I've ever heard—if you really mean it.'

'Oh, I mean it, sir! Ask any of the others. We've all seen her often enough, and you'll see her, too, sir. It sounds queer, I know, and it is queer, too—until you get used to it.'

Get used to it! I laughed out loud from sheer bewilderment, wondering what had bewitched my gardeners. I no more suspected that he might be telling me the truth than I believed that he was intentionally lying.

'Aren't you afraid of her?' I asked.

'Well, sir, 'tis a bit awesome-like, but none of us is afraid—not unless we've been doing something we didn't ought. For Miss Jessica knows. She could read most of a man's heart in life; and there's nothing hidden from her now. Young King—there's no harm in me telling you the story, sir, for it's all come right and he married the girl. But before he did he met Miss Jessica one evenin' in the alley over yonder. We'd seen her afore, but that night he lay in a dead faint for more 'n an hour. He said as her eyes burnt into the very soul of him like acid. '

I was still puzzled, of course, and amused, and on the whole well pleased. If my gardeners had invented for themselves an accusing conscience, so much the better. It induced them to do their work well and lead regular lives.

'Well, we'll extend that lawn,' I said, 'and if Miss Jessica minds, you come and tell me. '

Then I went indoors to tell Joan about it.

Joan was amused and highly delighted.

'How thrilling!' she said, I'm awfully pleased! A ghost makes an old house seem so much more complete, doesn't it?'

You may gather from that that Joan no more believed in such things than I did. We both waited with a great deal of amusement for Hudson to tell us that the spirit of his late mistress objected to the extension of the lawn, thereby saving him and his underlings some extra labour. But nothing of the sort occurred. Indeed, the new turf was being laid when I mentioned the matter tentatively to Hudson, and he told me that 'Miss Jessica didn't seem to mind'. Not very seriously, I expressed my gratitude to Miss Jessica, and I was distinctly puzzled I could no longer believe that her ghost had been invented as an excuse for avoiding difficult and arduous work.

Then one evening, about a fortnight later, I had the shock and surprise of my life.

On the south side of the house there is a long, straight walk, a narrow alley between hedges, a high one of hornbeam and a lower one of box which is always kept scrupulously clipped. Bays have been cut in the box hedge every few yards, and a garden seat placed in each of them. The alley ends where two paths branch off at right angles, and at the top, looking down the whole length of the walk, is a summer-house which, at that time of the year, was clustered all over with red rambler roses.

It was after dinner, but not yet dusk. Middle twilight, I think, is as good a description as any I can think of. Joan and I had dined alone, and I had lingered on in the dining-room for a little while after she had left me, and then taken a cigar with me into the alley for a quiet walk and a smoke in the calm, evening air.

I was thinking of nothing very definite or exciting, pacing slowly and with my gaze bent downwards. I was within ten yards of the end, where the summer-house stood, when I happened to raise my eyes, and I then saw the figure of a woman with her back turned towards me. She was rather tall, slim, and graceful, and seemed to be dressed in some soft grey material. Her neck was slightly bent, and I had the impression that she was in the act of savouring, or examining closely, a spray of roses by the summer-house door.

Strangely enough, I didn't at once think of the stories I had heard about Miss Jessica. I can't say exactly what I did think, but I naturally wondered who she was. We had nobody staying with us at the time, and she certainly was not a servant. I coughed, and she straightened herself at once, turned slowly, and looked at me, revealing herself full-faced.

I thought my heart had stopped for ever, before it gave a great bound and began to race. There was no longer any doubt as to who she was. In every cottage in the neighbourhood there was at least one photograph of Miss Jessica; and it was she who now faced me in the twilight.

Yes, of course I was afraid, but I really think I was still more bewildered. I was face to face with what I had hitherto regarded as the impossible. And now all the power of my startled eyes was focused upon her I could see that she was not of flesh and blood. I don't mean that she was diaphanous or semi-transparent; I mean—and this is rather hard to describe—that she seemed somehow fainter, less substantial, than an ordinary person seen at that distance would normally appear.

I don't know how long we faced each other motionless. Her face was very placid, her eyes thoughtful and kind, as if she were reading me. Instinct made me afraid, and yet instinct assured me that I had nothing to fear. At last—it seems odd to tell about it—I bowed to her. I had a queer, sheepish feeling that I had neglected this courtesy over long, and must have looked like a great ungainly schoolboy, suddenly remembering his manners. She returned this unspoken salutation in kind with an old-world air, an inimitable graceful dignity, and, reading as I think my unreasoning discomfort in her presence, turned slowly and walked down the path on the left, so that in a moment the hornbeam hedge hid her from view.

For some minute fraction of time I stood staring at the spot where she had stood; then I went swiftly to the top of the walk, and looked down the path which she had taken. It was a long, straight path ending in an arch which gave access to one of the lawns, and there was no one there. Well, I suppose a lot of men would have accused themselves of dreaming, but I didn't. I knew myself better than that. I had seen her. And she had seen me and read me! She had read the fear in my heart, and had gone quietly out of my presence in a normal manner to avoid further disturbing me by brushing past me or vanishing before my eyes. This, I know, savours of the ludicrous, but it's just what happened.

I went back to the house pretty thoughtfully, I can tell you. All my theories were upset. Ghosts certainly existed, because I had just seen one. Beyond all doubt there was a life after death, in which my belief had previously been lukewarm—a tacit acceptance with certain reservations of the teachings of the Established Church. I told Joan what had happened, and, of course, she laughed at me.

She laughed at me off and on for three days, and then she had just such an experience herself.

She saw Miss Jessica, one evening, among the tulips in the little sunk Dutch garden—saw at a distance an unfamiliar figure, thought at first that somebody had moved one of the stone gods, and went close to see. She was, I think, less disturbed than I was.

'I don't care,' said Joan. 'She's a dear. There's nothing whatever to be afraid of. I should have been scared to death if she'd been horrible and wicked I wonder what she wants?'

Well, we haven't found out what she wants, and I don't suppose we ever shall. Joan actually asked her once—I think I told you that we saw her several times after that—but had only a smile in reply. My own theory is that the one strain of innocent earthiness in this little lady kept her close after death to the gardens she had so loved in life.

So there it was. We had a ghost, and we soon grew accustomed to the thought of her. We knew that we had nothing to fear; that the little grey spirit which roamed about our gardens at dusk was beautiful and innocent and harmless. But that, I know now, was only because she saw no evil in us. Joan, of course, is the best woman in the whole world; and I—well, I've never meaningly done anybody a bad turn.

But we were soon to learn that, in the presence of evil, Miss Jessica was able to manifest herself in quite another way.

After the London season we had some people down to stay with us. They were nearly all Joan's sister's friends; not my kind of people. Joan and I are both simple, quiet-living folk. We don't need to be told that we're survivors of the Victorian era; nor, when told, do we take it as an insult. But we've given up being surprised at the manners and morals of the new generation. Half the people we had to ask were strangers to us, and we should have been content for them to have remained strangers.

You don't need me to describe the crowd of people which overran Wychfold for a few days. You know the sort: noisy, nerve-ridden, restless, and ill-mannered; painted girls with their painted mothers; men who would have been called cads a short while ago, who now went everywhere. By Jove, they were a mob! They might have sprung straight from the imagination of the late Father Vaughan. Not only the men drank too much, jokes passed muster which would have been frowned at in an East End bar; in every innuendo there was something sinister or vile; and gambling and talk of gambling went on throughout their waking hours. They played bridge and poker for ruinous stakes; they gambled on shots at golf, sets of tennis, everything possible for wagering; outrageous flirtations begun elsewhere were continued quite openly. As for ourselves, we couldn't do anything. If one has guests one must treat them in the way they expect to be treated, or let them do as they like. Joan and I were kept perpetually on thorns, but we had to grin and bear it.

Among these unwelcome guests was a fellow named Chaffneigh. I knew nothing whatever about him, somebody had 'brought' him. He held a commission as captain in a crack regiment, and he was a tall man in the middle thirties who looked ten years younger and carried his dissipations as a clever woman carries her age. He was, I soon gathered, part of the luggage with which Mrs Lawson-Endell and her daughter Phyllis had been travelling of late. At first I gave the fellow the small credit of thinking it was the mother he was after.

Mrs Lawson-Endell was a woman of—how old shall I say? At least she was old enough to have a daughter of about twenty. Nature had meant her to be plump, and to some extent she had erred in fighting Nature. Her figure was good. At a short distance she looked a girl; at close range she had—to quote the late Henry James—'a certain cadaverous beauty'.

Phyllis was a younger edition of her mother, a true product of an age in which affected innocence is out of date. She was pretty enough, and to my mind her paint and powder and face-creams were all unnecessary. But I liked her better than I liked most of the others, for I thought she was wholesome enough at core, and nothing worse than the victim of environment.

Well, I thought at first that Chaffneigh was after mamma, until I noticed that Phyllis and he were often tete-a-tete together, and often missing for noticeable periods. Then, being innocent, and—as I have been told—an embodiment of all the middle-class virtues, I thought that Chaffneigh was wooing the girl in the way of marriage. It was a cynical old devil named Cledge who undeceived me.

'I suppose,' I said to him casually, 'we shall hear an announcement from those two before long.'

Cledge rolled a cold, blue eye on me.

'What sort of an announcement?' he asked.

'Well, it looks to me as if they're both serious.'

Cledge laughed aloud at that.

'Possibly,' he said, 'if Chaffneigh weren't already married   '

'Is he?'

'Not very noticeably, I grant you, but married all the same. He rarely sees his wife, never talks about her, and I don't suppose he ever thinks about her. One thing I'll say for Chaffneigh, he's not morbid.'

'Then what's he doing running after Phyllis?'

'Oh, well, of course' Cledge shrugged his shoulders. 'It's very regrettable, I know. But you must admit he doesn't have to run far.'

'It's a nice state of affairs,' I muttered. 'Does Phyllis know?'

'About Mrs Chaffneigh? Everybody does. Don't look so horrified. Phyllis is Chaffneigh's latest. I don't suppose she'll last more than a month or two. Girls of about that age are his hobby.'

My eyes must have been opening wider and wider.

'But why on earth does her mother allow it?' I wanted to know. Cledge laughed again; a thin, rattling laugh which jarred on me.

'I should like to see mamma,' he said, 'doing the heavy, virtuous, Victorian parent. Do you think Phyllis doesn't know about her mother? Que voulez-vous? Like mother, like daughter, I suppose. You didn't think Mrs Lawson-Endell was a second Caesar's wife, did you?'

'I didn't know'

'My dear fellow, Cleopatra herself wouldn't have received the woman. We're not living in an age of grace, you know.'

'So I am beginning to be aware. I should never have called myself a prude, but—damn it all! When I was a young man a married woman was expected to take care of herself, but a young girl'

'Other times, other manners. I don't hold with cradle-snatching myself. I know when we were young Chaffneigh would have been barred by everybody—which would have been rather a pity, because I find him amusing. But I shouldn't worry about it, if I were you. You won't have this crowd around your neck forever. Do your best to put up with them for a day or two, and say thank Heaven when they're gone. By the way, who's the lady in old-fashioned grey togs I ran into yesterday evening? She looks the summit of respectability. You haven't got somebody here who's been so scared by her fellow-guests that she's retired to her room and stayed there? Because I haven't seen her about the house.'

'Whom do you mean?' I asked.

'How on earth should I know whom I mean? I met her on one of the garden paths last night—white-haired, but quite a young face. Very old-fashioned style of woman, prim as a Scots elder. Stared at me as if I were the villain of a Lyceum melodrama. Made me turn creepy all over; so much so that I sneaked back to the billiards-room and took a large dose of alcoholic poison.'

I knew at once whom he meant and blurted out thoughtlessly; 'That was a ghost you saw, Cledge!'

Naturally he didn't take me seriously.

'Oh, was it? Well, she certainly behaved like one. Daresay if we investigate we should find she was the housekeeper's sister or something, although she didn't look like it.'

Well, I didn't say another word on that subject to old Cledge. I didn't want my guests to start a ghost hunt. I could well imagine the spirit in which such an undertaking would be carried out. And there was something incongruous in the thought of people like Chaffneigh and the Lawson-Endells encountering the gentle spirit of Miss Jessica. Poor little lady, I wondered what she thought of those guests of mine.

I took the opportunity of having a quiet word with Joan that evening, and went into her room while she was dressing for dinner. Her hair was already done, and in response to a glance from me she sent the maid away. I sat down on the edge of the bed, and told her all that I had learned from Cledge. Joan felt exactly as I did.

'But I don't see what we can do,' she said I'm having some of my purgatory now. I shall be the happiest woman in the world when they're gone.'

'I thought,' I suggested awkwardly, 'if you were to say a word or two to the girl, perhaps?'

'What can I say? She'd only laugh at me. That chit is a woman of the world in her way. And besides, she's got a mother to look after her.'

'Yes,' I agreed bitterly, 'she's got a mother.'

'Well, it's only for a day or two,' said Joan with a sigh of resignation.

But the party was destined to break up earlier than we had expected. It was about an hour after dinner on that same evening, and after a short forgathering in the drawing-room, our guests proceeded to follow their own devices. There was a bridge table going, and some pretty free criticism between partners. After a little while, Cledge and I wandered into the billiard-room.

The long windows of the billiard-room overlook the south side, and the billiard-room is separated from the gun-room by a narrow passage ending in a door which opens on to the terrace. Cledge said he would like a game, and as the shaded lights over the table were strong, and the mingling of bluish twilight from outside was scarcely noticeable, we did not draw the blinds. We played in a desultory fashion, chatting between the strokes, and often making long pauses between them.

'Where's Chaffneigh?' I asked.

Cledge missed a follow-through cannon, and, still leaning over the table with his cue poised, made a faint grimace.

'Where was Mary's lamb? Tell me where Phyllis is, and I'll have a good guess.'

'It's a damn shame!' I said.

'Well, don't worry about it. Worry cramps a man's style for billiards.

You ought to get thirty or forty here. I think I'll sit down.'

He sat down and I went to the table and played an easy losing hazard off the red. I had hardly completed the stroke when Cledge was upon his legs once more.

'What the' I heard him exclaim.

He was staring out of the window where the last of the daylight still struggled with the dusk. I could hear a blundering of light footfalls from out on the terrace, and as my gaze followed the direction of Cledge's I saw Phyllis running past the windows. She was swaying like a sail in the wind, and her hands were pressed to her eyes, covering her face. For a moment she withdrew them and even in that dim light I saw that her face was livid, tear-stained, twisted, and wrung by some unbearable emotion.

'Here, what's happened?' said Cledge in an undertone. 'Where's Chaffneigh?'

I was already half-way to the door, and I had hardly reached it when I heard the girl enter by the door from the terrace; I heard her sobbing and gasping as if she had just beaten Death by a short head in some ghastly race; and I went round into the passage to meet her. I shall never forget the sight of her and the way she behaved. She fawned on me with her hands like a child, and then clutched me around the shoulders as if she were drowning. Cledge went into the gun-room and brought back some brandy in a tumbler. She shook her head at it at first, but after a while I got her to sip a little.

'What's the matter, Phyllis?' I asked, as gently as my shaken voice would let me. 'Where's Chaffneigh?'

'He's with her. I've been a beast and a fool. She saw and she made me see. She saw me as I am with those eyes of hers'

A fit of shuddering seized the girl from head to foot. Over her shoulders Cledge was framing words at me with his lips. 'Nerves, breakdown,' he was trying to say. I took no heed of him.

'Whom are you speaking of?' I asked. 'Come, tell me.'

'I don't know who she is I was sitting with Captain Chaffneigh in the summer-house at the top of the alley. She isn't a woman. She's something fine—and terrible—and just!'

I gave her another sip of brandy.

'Do try' to pull yourself together, my dear,' I muttered, 'and try to tell us just what happened.'

She shuddered again.

'I don't care,' she stammered. 'Why shouldn't I tell you? She knows! Captain Chaffneigh was asking me to run away with him. And—and I know I was going to. And we both looked up, and there she was standing before us, with her white hair and face that was sweet and yet terrible, and her eyes that burned into my heart like red-hot irons. She couldn't have heard more than a word or two, but I knew she knew. She knew everything, I tell you, every thought in my mind that nobody else has a right to know. My soul was naked before those eyes of hers, and in a moment I saw it as she saw it. I'm a beast—no, far worse than a beast! I'm not fit to—not fit to'

She swallowed heavily and began to cry again.

'The lady didn't speak?' I asked, with a queer tremor in my voice.

'No. She only—she only looked. There was no need to speak. Oh, let me go! I'm not fit to be touched.'

'Don't be a silly child. Where is Chaffneigh?'

'With her.'

'With her?'

She had hidden her face again and for the moment only nodded heavily.

At last she stammered in a muffled voice:

'I ran away and left them. She meant me to. They were standing face to face, and his was white—white like chalk.'

I didn't know at the time what Cledge was thinking of all of this, but at that moment his hand closed on my arm and his voice breathed in my ear.

'Here's Chaffneigh! For Heaven's sake, get her away quick!'

So I dragged the shrinking, trembling girl into the hall and called for Joan. I left her sobbing on Joan's shoulder, declaring that she was not fit to touch anybody who was good. I should have left them together in any case, but Cledge precipitated my departure by charging madly up the passage from the gun-room and calling to me:

'Come on, man! Chaffneigh!'

I heard Chaffneigh before I reached him. He was raving like one possessed by a devil. And the sight of the man appalled me. He had got hold of a bottle of brandy—drinks were always left ready to hand in the gun-room—and the edge of a tumbler clattered against his teeth as he tried to drink. His face was as white as paper, ghastly, awful, stamped by the seal of fear and something worse. It might have served a painter for the model of a reprobate being thrust into the pit.

Cledge and I got hold of him and loosened his collar. We tried to get him to tell us what was wrong.

'She told me—she told me' was all he could say. He could get no further than that.

What 'she' told him we shall never know. Perhaps she told him without speech what he was and what was immediately to happen to him. For something did happen to him.

Suddenly his white face darkened with a flood of colour, and in a moment he was writhing in a fit. And in that fit he died a few seconds later.

And that is the whole story—every word of it. For obvious reasons I haven't told you the real names of the people concerned, but anybody who is curious can find out if they care to take the trouble.

So we know that the gentle little spirit of Miss Jessica is not always gentle. If either of us had cause to be afraid of her we should not live at Wychfold.

As for Phyllis, she is an enigma to all but the one or two who know the story. She is a changed character, and is engaged to a parson—of all people!—who has a working-class parish. For obvious reasons we don't like to ask her down again. I don't think she'd care to risk facing Miss Jessica a second time, although I think Miss Jessica would now look kindly on her, perhaps with the shadow of a smile, and move quickly out of her presence as if she were shy.

## The Lady of Graeme

I met a lady in the meads,
Full beautiful, a faery "s child;
Her hair was long, her foot was light,
And her eyes were wild.

Keats

I walked up from the station to Donald's place, although the distance was two miles, and my privileged friends were wont to call me lazy to my face. There were two reasons for this excess of energy, and I admit that the greater was because there was no sort of conveyance from the Hall to meet me. The other was that I was not averse from a walk by myself through the spinney where the bodies had been found. A halfpenny newspaper, in 'booming' the mystery, had obligingly published a rough sketch map of Donald's estate, so that I was not in much danger of losing my way.

Donald did not expect me until the last train meandered into Brimpley Station at something to eleven, but I had arrived at Charing Cross before my time and found that the previous train (late as usual) had not yet started. Hence my early arrival, and no Donald nor any high-powered car to meet

It was a fine starlit night, with the closeness of thunder in the air, but nothing in the sky to suggest that a storm was imminent, and there was a friendly smell of mown hay and cattle, grateful to the nostrils of a jaded Londoner. I left my luggage at the station, telling the porter-stationmaster-cum-signalman that it would probably be called for that same night, if not, early the next morning; then I walked up a narrow passage into the village street, and was probably taken for a newspaper reporter by such natives as happened to be up and out. That village was crowded with newspaper men, some of them openly admitting their calling, others disguised as artists.

My way took me right through the village, which consisted only of one street, and then about a mile up the London road, until, having climbed a stile and set foot on a path leading diagonally across a long meadow, I was at last upon Donald's land.

In spite of a certain knowledge of the Unseen, I was not a particularly imaginative person, and, strange to say, although I was close to the scene of the weird mystery that had set all England talking, I gave the matter scarcely a thought as I trudged along.

My mind dwelt largely upon Donald and our long friendship, and the changes that time had wrought upon ourselves.

We had both been very poor, we had both raised ourselves from cheap and nasty schools by sheer hard work, and our friendship had begun when we shared a study as scholarship boys at Cranberg. It was curious to think how he, the gentleman, good at games as well as in the classroom, and I, the 'outsider', notable only as a 'swot', remained inseparable through the changes and rough-and-tumble of six years of public school life; and how afterwards for four more years we had borrowed shillings off each other and drunk each other's cocoa when we were scholarship men at a small Oxford college.

After we had come down Donald obtained a junior mastership at Cranberg, and somehow contrived to support his mother on what he earned. Then, suddenly, a twentieth century miracle happened, and he, only a cadet of the Graeme family, found himself head of the house, rich, master of wide estates in Kent. Fortune had no plums for me. I continued to earn only a sufficiency of bread and butter as science master at a suburban institute, but I did not envy Donald. He was a good fellow, and deserved his luck; moreover, he was still the same to his oldest friend. I got long letters from him every week and impulsively-worded invitations; but this was the first time he had ever lured me to Graeme Hall, and now I went only because he was in trouble and had need of me.

Yes, I was thinking of Donald and old times more than of the strange deaths that had occurred on the Graeme estate, and the weird legend connected with the Graemes, which the papers were then turning into copious copy. My head was tired with puzzling over the strange business. I had, as it were, dipped my little finger into occultism, and knew just sufficient to be assured of the existence of an unseen world with powerful forces for good and evil; but I was at the same time so hard-headed as to be sceptical in particular cases.

I have said that the night was starlit. There was, however, no moon, and light as it was on the road and in the open fields, darkness crept round me directly I entered the first thicket through which I had to pass. For a long while I met nobody, although I fully expected a number of adventurers to be up and watching, since the roads and footpaths through the Graeme estate were open to the public.

At last, when I had crossed the ornamental wooden bridge over the trout-stream, and saw the darkness of trees in front of me, I knew that I was about to enter the spinney where the dead had been found.

Then, indeed, something around my heart seemed to tighten, and a spasm of nervousness passed over me. I found, rather to my annoyance, that I possessed an imagination, and the fancy took me that a deeper hush lay over the earth—that all Nature was listening and waiting for something to happen.

The trees, I imagined against my will, were conscious of my presence, and expressed their emotions towards me in the various attitudes in which they had grown. One leaned forward in tense expectation, as if it whispered 'Hush!' to its fellows. Another was silently derisive, as if it knew of some huge joke in preparation for me, and enjoyed the spectacle of my walking blindly into the trap. A third was very old and very evil, a Caliban among trees.

Of course, I was well aware that these fancies proceeded from disordered nerves, and I had to keep a tight hold on myself to prevent my mind from creating more unpleasant things. For all that, I could not help thinking that my footsteps, ringing out clearly on a hard path, were advertising my presence to something evil that lurked in the trees. I walked a little more softly, feeling compelled to make at least that concession to my weaker nature.

The spinney was crowded thickly with trees on either side of the path. Over the path a ragged channel of sky was visible. To right and left the ground sloped upward at a gentle angle. There was no sound anywhere save that of my own cautious footsteps.

She was the most beautiful woman I had ever seen.

I write thus of her coming, because at the time I was aware of her beauty before I was aware of her *presence.* I did not see her come, but she was walking beside me when some veil over my senses had been lifted. She was walking beside me and smiling.

She wore a white robe of some clinging soft material, almost transparent, and it showed the graceful outlines of her form. The way she walked was a pure joy to behold, and no twigs cracked beneath her little white feet.

Her hair was long and black, and fell down her back in soft waves to below the waist line. Her eyes were black, too, and they smiled, or rather, leered invitation, and hinted at slyness and evil They were the vilest and most lovely eyes I have ever seen. Her features, to describe them as a whole, had that strange spirit-beauty with which painters endow nymphs, but a greater beauty than I have ever seen upon canvas or on a human face. Strangest of all was the colour of her skin, which was a silvery white, like the moon on a clear evening—an almost leprous whiteness, and in contrast her full lips were redder than blood.

Looking back, it seems strange to me that her eyes and mouth did not shock me into fear, for if her eyes were evil her mouth was that of a devil. The upper lip was raised a little, the lower sucked in, and her teeth looked out white and sharp. This when she smiled, and she was smiling all the while with a hideous cunning and a viciousness only half-concealed.

I was not afraid, although her very vileness was undisguised. I think she was too horrible and too lovely to fear. I went on walking, and she kept pace beside me, her eyes gloating on mine, while all Nature watched and listened.

Suddenly I stopped, and she, too, was still. I trembled, and gazed upon her with an insane desire to kiss that evil mouth. She knew, for her lips pouted as if they would be kissed. There stole upon my senses hot, sweet perfumes and wondrous melodies. I opened my arms like a child, and held them out to her.

Dreams stranger and more beautiful than are vouchsafed to the opium slave became mine at the touching of our lips. I was swooning—slow-ly—very slowly. I felt the tide of life ebbing from my body, and I was well content to let it go. I heard the sound of rivers flowing, and on one of them I fancied myself to be drifting gently towards sleep.

A shrill scream pierced through the veil that wrapped around my senses. I became conscious once more, with something of the feeling of one coming suddenly to the surface of water after a deep dive. The woman was no longer there, and, strangely enough, it was then that I began to loathe and fear her. I felt terribly weak, and had some difficulty to stand upright.

The hush was broken now. All through the spinney there were sounds—the ordinary night sounds where there are trees and birds. There were also quick footsteps, and, turning, I beheld a little, short, thick-set man rushing towards me, and brandishing a thick ash stick. I knew instinctively that this was the man whose loud scream had broken the spell and brought me back to life.

'My God!' he cried, coming near. 'I thought—I thought. Where is she?'

His face was white, and he was sweating; he was in almost as bad a plight as myself.

'There is no one here,' I said, to soothe him.

'I know—I know! But just now—I could have sworn I saw her—all in white—in your arms—and her beautiful, beastly face-'

He looked wildly around him, and I had time to recover myself and bestow upon him a closer scrutiny. I had no doubt that he was either a detective or a newspaper man, and in either case I preferred to deceive him.

'Look here,' I said, 'you've been dreaming. There's been nobody here except myself. You must have been imagining things.'

'Eh?' He looked up at me a little relieved, I thought. 'I could have sworn—but you ought to know, of course. This place has got on my nerves a bit, and I'm going to chuck it for the night. I'm not going to risk my reason for three pounds ten a week, to say nothing of my life. I say—you a pressman?'

I shook my head.

'No, a friend of Mr Graeme.'

'Oh! I was going to ask you not to tell the others, if you were. My name's Rumbold—of the *Daily Visitor*. I say'—he harked back—'even now I can hardly believe that there was no one—my nerves must be rotten!'

He ended with a weak laugh, and looked at me a little suspiciously, I thought. The man irritated me, and I was anxious for him to go so that I might think.

'Let me walk with you up to the top of the spinney,' he babbled on. 'Then I'll get back. I— I've had enough of being by myself. Five men dead here in a month, and that beastly legend! I say, you're a bit shaky, too!'

'Oh,' I answered, with all the nonchalance at my command, 'I don't pretend to have iron nerves. You startled me, you know, when you yelled out. Yes, by all means let's walk up to the top together. Have you been wandering about here long? Not much copy, I'm afraid.'

He shrugged his shoulders.

'I don't know. Tomorrow morning I shall know better what I've imagined and what I haven't. In spite of what you tell me I'm not at all sure that I haven't saved your life. D'you mind telling me your name, sir?'

'No, you don't,' I answered. 'I don't want to become famous through this affair.'

Rumbold nodded. He was recovering rapidly from his fright, and his professional instincts were fast asserting themselves.

'I shall call you Smith,' he said. 'After all, you are more likely to be Smith than anyone else. Ah, look ahead! We're almost out of this beastly spinney, and I'm not sorry for it, either.'

We were almost out, but not quite. Whilst talking we had fallen into a quick step, jogging along together side by side in the gloom. Ahead was a break in the trees filled in with the silvery light of the stars shining on wide pastures. Another ten yards would have taken us out into the open when Rumbold tripped and fell. His scream was a veritable nightmare sound, and seemed to fill the air with fear.

I stooped, and in spite of the nausea forcing up my gorge, managed to lift him off the dead body which had tripped him up.

I saw at once that the man was quite dead. I knew the yellow face and the sad smile of death too well. He was quite young and rather handsome, and he lay on his back in the posture of one asleep.

'It's Warne!' Rumbold panted in my ear. 'Warne, of the *Evening Comet*. I knew him well. We did a holiday together once.'

'Look here,' I said, very slowly and distinctly, 'the sooner we do something the better. If you come out into the open you can watch the body from there. Are you afraid of being left alone for a short while?'

'Not out in the open.'

'All right. Then I'll go up to the Hall and tell Mr Graeme, and he'll phone for the police. We'll be with you very soon. Keep steady, man! Or would you rather I stopped and you went up to the house?'

He shook his head. His fear seemed to have passed and left him dazed and stupid.

'Warne,' he muttered, 'quite a good chap—we did a holiday together once.'

'By Jove!' exclaimed Donald in that hushed voice of his that sounded so much more emotional than even a woman's scream.

It was two hours later. The police had come and gone, but we supposed them still to be searching the grounds. The body of the unfortunate man had been carried away. We were smoking over the very needful glasses of whisky in the library, and Donald had just heard my story, much as I have set it down in these pages.

'What was she like?' he asked.

I tried to describe her, and failed. It would have needed a new language. No master painter could have depicted her beauty, and Aubrey Beardsley could not have portrayed a tithe of her vileness.

Donald poured himself out another drink, sipped it, and began to pace the room.

'Bill,' he said, 'I believe if this goes on it will send me mad, and I'll either put myself out of the way in as clean a manner as possible or go out into the spinney one night and let that damned hag do her worst. If I'd dreamed of all the trouble that was to come to me with the money I should have renounced my claim. You know how I hate publicity, and the eyes of England are glued on me and my little bit of land. '

'It must all come to an end soon,' I began, with an effort at speaking cheerfully.

'Why?' he asked bluntly.

'If only people would keep out of the spinney! Fear will drive them away in time  '

'But people won't keep away!' he cried. 'Some laugh at the story of the woman, and go there out of bravado. Others believe—and the odd part is that they're tempted to go, in spite of funking it. I—I've wanted to go out there to my death. I've seemed to hear her infernal witch's voice calling me. And it's me she wants more than all the others, Bill.'

I watched him narrowly, and more than a little anxiously. He looked wasted and ill, but his face was flushed, and I guessed that he was in a state of fever through excitement and anxiety.

'I'm glad you're here,' he went on presently. 'If you only knew what a relief it is to have old Bill about the house!' He smiled. 'I've got used to you, Bill, you know.' Then he went off at a tangent. 'I say, you had a narrow shave tonight. You're the only one who's seen her and lived! That chap Rumbold saved your life. If—if anything had happened to you I think I should just have gone out and let her kiss my life away under the trees. D'you know, Bill, you're the only pal I've got, barring the mater and Joyce.' He gave me a sidelong glance as the latter name came hesitatingly from his lips. I did not know who Joyce was, but I asked no questions, being well assured that Donald would tell me in his own good time 'Look here,' I said, 'do you feel like going to bed?'

He made a negative gesture.

'No, I'm hanged if I do. Do you?'

I shook my head.

'That being so,' I went on, 'I should like you to tell me the legend which all the papers have been publishing in connection with the—the deaths on your land. I've read about a dozen accounts, and they're all different.'

Donald nodded.

'The papers got it all wrong, as usual,' he said. He sat down in an uncomfortable posture on the arm of a chair. 'There are lots of versions of the story even in this neighbourhood,' he went on, 'but this couplet lies at the root of them all. It is a sort of foundation for half a dozen legends:

"Many shall die on the lands of Graeme
When the Lady of Spells shall come again." '

'It sounds a genuine old couplet,' I said. 'The rhyming's so bad. And the legends?'

'None of them very different from each other. You can tell that they all come from the same well-spring; but the story has passed from generation to generation, and some say this and others that. The most popular story is that about three hundred years ago a woodman and his daughter lived on the land here when my ancestor, Daniel Graeme, was head of the family. This girl was reputed a witch at a period when any beautiful girl or very ugly old woman enjoyed the same reputation. Perhaps because all the people around were fairly prosperous, and nothing went wrong with the crops and cattle, she escaped the ducking stool and the faggots. The girls and young men used to come to her for love-philtres, and she was said to possess the gift of reading the future in well-water.

'In those days, of course, it wasn't considered infra dig for the lord of the manor to philander with the girls on his estate. If he didn't, his friends considered either that he had puritan tendencies or that he was afraid of his wife. It was the right thing to do. Daniel Graeme hadn't a wife to be afraid of, and psalm-singers over at Maidstone used to compare him unfavourably with the Pope.

'Whether or not the little woodman's daughter was a witch, she certainly cast a spell over Daniel. He seems to have been some hundreds of years ahead of his time in that he promised to marry her. It was unnecessary in those days. Village girls did not expect it, but Daniel promised.

'If the girl could read other people's futures in the well, she could not read her own. She built all her hopes on being lady of the manor, and, of course, Daniel never kept his promise. Her love is supposed to have turned to a most bitter hatred, and, so the legend goes, she refused all religious aid in her last moments, saying that she was tokened to the devil, who would help her to be revenged on the house of Graeme. She died after giving birth to a daughter.

'Now, this daughter died at the age of three years, and before her death she made a prophecy that sounded strange upon the lips of a child. She is reputed to have spoken the rhyme I have just told you The interpretation generally placed upon it is that one day the soul of the witch-girl will be born again and weak death and destruction on the land of which she thought to become mistress. That's the story as near as I can discover. What d'you make of it, Bill?'

I said nothing for a long while. It was not a very uncommon story. Every landed family can boast of a legend of the same kind, some of half a dozen. I was not absurdly credulous, but where there was smoke I was ever in search of fire. At least, I had good cause for knowing that some occult evil influence was at work. Why should not the legend and the prophecy be true? Why should not the Thing which had so nearly caused my death in the spinney be the reincarnation of the witch-girl betrayed by Donald's ancestor? Witches? People who know everything will tell you that there never were, nor could be, such things. I have seen what I have seen even in this, the hard-headed, hard-hearted 20th century. What of the women in the Tudor and Stuart periods who actually confessed to being witches, and did not deny the extraordinary evidence brought against them, although the punishment was death by burning?

'How many men have met their death in the spinney?' I asked presently.

'That poor fellow Warne makes the seventh,' Donald answered. 'You've been reading the papers—you know as much about that part of the affair as I do. No marks of violence, and on the first two the coroner's jury brought in verdicts of "Death from natural causes". Heart failure, was the general opinion Then it became something more than a coincidence, and the jury brought in an open verdict on the third and on the three successive cases. Then the papers got hold of it, and dug up the legend, and—oh, if you only knew how sick I am of it all! I'm sorry for the poor devils who're dead, but it's the horror of the thing that affects me so. And I've got other worries, too. There's Joyce, you know, and the mater, and—oh, I forgot! I haven't told you about Joyce yet. I'm wool-gathering tonight.'

He poured himself out another stiff dose of whisky. I looked rather pointedly at the glass as he took it over to the syphon.

'I shouldn't,' I said

He laughed rather nervously.

'It's all right, old man. You needn't think I've taken to this sort of thing. But I want something tonight. My nerves are rotten—putrid! I say, Bill, you are going to back me up, aren't you?'

He was vague, but I managed to make an answer that satisfied him.

'I mean about this ghastly business in the spinney,' he explained after a long drink. 'You'll help me tackle it. You know something of occultism. It isn't natural for things to walk that ought to be lying still. There are ways of getting them back to the grave again.'

'Yes,' I answered, 'there are ways, but they are sometimes dangerous ways. You know you can count on me.'

'And not only that,' he said, 'but you'll help me about Joyce—Oh, I forgot again—haven't told you about Joyce. You won't sympathise, old chap, because you never did care for girls. But you'll help me all the same, I know.'

I smiled to myself. It was no new thing for Donald to be in love. Like most young men who are good-looking, jolly, and athletic, he had been in the habit of falling in and out of love with a bewildering frequency. At school there was the daughter of a confectioner, who subsequently gave place to a lady in a tobacconist's at Oxford, and while he was a master at Cranberg, 'old Graeme's fillies' provided table conversations for the boys when all other subjects had been discussed threadbare.

He saw the smile, and presently his own lips broadened.

'I know what you're thinking,' he said, 'but it's serious this time. I never knew what love was until I met Joyce. You'll see her tomorrow, and you'll understand. The trouble is that the mater is—well, a bit ambitious for me.'

He lit a cigarette.

'When I was a master at Cranberg,' he went on, 'the mater wouldn't have made any fuss about Joyce. Now I'm a poor devil of a squire she thinks no girl under the rank of a princess is good enough for me. It took me all my time to get her to call on Joyce, and if she guessed that I was a bit keen on her she wouldn't have gone. Joyce is as well-bred as any girl you'd wish to meet, but she isn't "county". As a matter of fact she's in an office in town, and she's stopping at a farmhouse down here for the sake of her health. She's just had something very like a nervous breakdown, poor kid.'

I nodded. 'But I don't see how I can help you there,' I said.

'You can with the mater,' he answered. 'She's got an awful respect for your judgment. If you crack Joyce up, the mater'll think the world of her.'

I promised, of course. I would have promised anything that night in the hope of cheering Donald up.

'Do you mind if I ask if there is any understanding between you?' I said. Donald made a gesture of uncertainty.

'I haven't said anything to her,' he answered, 'but I expect she guesses. I think she cares for me. I should be happy if it weren't for—for this other horrible business. But now you're here—somehow you've got a wonderful knack of saying nothing and making a fellow believe it'll all come right in the end. I say, you'd like to turn in, wouldn't you? And you've got no togs for the night until your luggage comes up. Come to my room, and I'll lend you some pyjamas.'

'That's a good idea,' I said, I'm beginning to feel a bit sleepy. By the way—just one thing. Why don't you close the grounds for the present, until all this is over?'

Donald finished off his drink and set the glass down upon the tray. 'Because,' he said, 'there are rights of way all over the property. The land belongs almost as much to the British public as it does to me. The people who don't wash their necks and enjoy holding forth in marketplaces would be up in arms. They'd enjoy pulling down the gates and doing a war-dance through my preserves. If they want to come and die mysteriously, they'll have to. I can't keep 'em out. Ready, Bill? I'm going to turn out the light.'

I did not meet Mrs Graeme until just before lunchtime on the following day. She rose very late, and was evidently in a poor state of health, which was little to be wondered at. Donald had already broken to her the tidings of poor Warne's death the night before, knowing that the knowledge could not escape her for long; but he had said nothing of my own experience, and warned me with a little nudge and a frown not to mention it.

I found her looking considerably older and less happy than in her days of poverty, but, chatting with me, she soon brightened up. It was quite obvious that she liked and trusted me, and was more inclined to rely on my judgment than on that of poor Donald. I waited impatiently for some reference to Joyce, and presently it came.

'There is a girl coming here to tea this afternoon,' she said, 'and I want you to have a good look at her, Bill, and tell me if you think her pretty.'

'I think,' I answered, 'that Donald is a much better judge of such matters. What does he think?'

'Donald? Oh, he's prejudiced. He's very much taken up with her.'

I glanced across at Donald, and saw that he was looking uneasy 'Still, I don't mind,' Mrs Graeme continued. 'Every young man likes a pretty girl to flirt with—except you, of course, Bill. And I know,' she added tentatively with a narrow look at her son, 'that my boy wouldn't do anything foolish, for his mother's sake.'

Donald grunted some monosyllable, and then went out of the room, remarking that he had something to say to the head gardener before the latter went off to his dinner. When we were alone together Mrs Graeme turned to me with her most confidential air.

'Bill,' she said, 'I'm so glad you came down. I feel I can rely on you. I know you're fond of dear old Donald, and would do anything to promote his ultimate happiness. I am afraid he has fallen in love.'

'I am very sorry,' I answered, 'if it is a case for fearing.'

She intertwined her long, narrow fingers, and leaned forward, rocking herself gently to and fro.

'I would sooner die,' she said, 'than stand in the way of my boy's happiness, and if the girl is really necessary to him I shall say nothing. But—I don't like her, Bill. There is something—I don't know what it is, but I am prejudiced. To begin with, she is not quite a lady, but that is only of secondary' importance. You will see her this afternoon. Her name is Joyce Parronage. She is the girl I spoke of just now.'

I nodded.

'Ah, yes. And you want to know if I think her pretty.'

'There is no doubt at all about that,' Mrs Graeme replied. 'She is—I was going to say devilishly pretty. What I want your opinion on is something much more important I want to know whether you think her nice—whether she will make dear old Donald happy. Your opinion of her will weigh a great deal with me. I used to listen quite gravely to your advice when you were a boy of twelve!'

'It may be less valuable now,' I laughed.

'No,' she answered, 'you've kept single, and you don't say very much. Those two characteristics in a man make women respect his judgments.'

At that moment the gong sounded, and Mrs Graeme went out on to the terrace to call Donald.

I met Joyce that afternoon, and a double surprise awaited me I expected to meet a fluffy, dolly little person, such as I believe frivolous young men would refer to as a 'pet'; but instead I was introduced to a tall, slim young woman with a face full of character as well as beauty.

'Better than pretty,' old Mrs Merritt afterwards whispered to me, and that was quite an adequate summing up of her appearance.

There were about half a dozen people in to tea, and when I entered the drawing-room the girl was being introduced to the two old sisters of the rector. I started at the sight of her, and felt my blood running cold, whilst my heart set up that dull, heavy thumping, which is one of the signals of fear. I thought myself mad for the moment, and exposed my indifferent breeding by fixing her with a long and searching stare. She was the beautiful and evil Thing that had so subtly attacked me in the spinney.

I thought that at first, and my brain reeled. Then I saw that I was mistaken. The spirit woman in the spinney had no corporeal being, whereas the girl who was now laughing with the two old maids over some feeble jest was almost strikingly material. Her face had little or none of the evil I had seen in the face which almost lured me to death, and certainly not all its beauty. But the resemblance was so extraordinary as momentarily to fill me with fear and deprive me of my manners.

Mrs Graeme looked rather queerly at me as she nodded for me to come up and be presented.

'Miss Parronage,' she said, 'I want to introduce Mr Hayling to you—a very old friend of Donald's.'

I bowed, and waited on the alert for the first sign of her offering her hand. She made a little tentative movement with an air of embarrassment and rather an awkward manner, and I took her hand and shook it. It may sound ridiculous, but I only half expected to touch warm and living flesh. What I had touched on the previous night was something that dissolved away in dreams and music.

She made no sign of having seen me before, and if her manner were slightly embarrassed I could see that it was only because she was not quite at home in a drawing-room like Mrs Graeme's. But her resemblance to the Thing that haunted the spinney was so strong even as I looked up at her then that I scarcely knew how to address her.

I muttered a how-d'ye-do, which coincided most ridiculously with a similar greeting from her lips, and got away from her as best I could, and, Mrs Graeme having sent away the servant, busied myself with helping Donald hand round the cups of tea and the microscopic cakes and sandwiches.

Presently Donald seated himself by Miss Parronage's side, and Mrs Merritt, an acquaintance of my early youth, made room for me beside her on a settee.

This distribution of her visitors did not please Mrs Graeme, and therefore it lasted only a few minutes. I could tell that she wanted me to talk to Miss Parronage, and presently she dexterously contrived for Donald and myself to change places. I sat down beside the girl with a set purpose in view, for I had been thinking while I pretended to listen to Mrs Merritt'schatter.

Fortunately she gave me the opening I wanted before I had spoken with her a minute.

'Are you stopping here very long?' she asked.

'I shouldn't think so,' I answered, 'although Mrs Graeme and Donald are very hospitable and persuasive. But I am a very busy man, and London calls me.'

'Ah,' she said, 'I, too, am a Londoner. I have come down here to get better. I have been very ill.'

'I hope,' said I, 'that you have already benefited by the change.'

She looked thoughtful. 'I think I have—in a way,' she said doubtfully. 'The air is very good here, and I can sleep. I could not sleep at all in town. Yes, I think that I am very' much better, really. Have you ever suffered from nerves and sleeplessness, Mr Hayling?'

'Quite enough to sympathise with you, Miss Parronage,' I answered.

She laughed. 'Oh, well, then, you know what it is.'

'Let's compare symptoms,' I suggested smiling.

'Well I couldn't sleep and felt run down and wretched, and the doctor said I'd been overworking, and told me to take a long rest in the country. So I came down here. The air here soon cured me of sleeplessness. The trouble is that here I sleep too much.'

'That's a fault on the right side, at any rate,' I laughed.

'Yes, perhaps. But I don't exactly mean that I sleep too much; I ought to have said too soundly. I don't sleep more than the usual seven or eight hours, but nothing will wake me in the night. A big picture fell down in the farmhouse where I am stopping a night or two ago, and it did not wake me. The farmer's wife knocked at my door to explain what had happened, in case I was frightened, but I did not hear her. The poor old thing got quite alarmed, and thought I was dead. '

I drew a quick breath that was almost an exclamation, and looked away, fearful lest she should have heard it.

'Do you—dream?' I asked presently, trying to speak in my ordinary voice.

'Oh, yes.' She shuddered, and nearly upset her cup of tea. 'Oh, yes, horrible dreams. I can't bear to speak of them. I—I don't quite remember what I have dreamed when I wake up, but something I can't quite recollect haunts me all day. I think I would sooner suffer from insomnia.'

I said the usual fatuous things while my mind was at work on a problem so horrible and bizarre that I had much ado to control my face. I seem to remember advising her to take plenty of exercise and not worry about anything, the sort of advice which doctors reel off parrot fashion to nervous patients. She recognised it, having paid good money to men with letters after their names for telling her the same thing.

'And eat plenty of eggs and vegetables,' she laughed, suddenly becoming frivolous. 'Don't forget to tell me when you have set up in practice, Dr Hayling, and I will be sure and come to you '

Fortunately, Donald would not be kept away from her for long. He came over and seated himself on the other side of her, and began chatting, so giving me the opportunity to sit by myself a little apart from the others and think.

My thinking was solely concerned with what was to be done, for I had already solved the mystery of the deaths on Donald's estate. Impossible as it seemed, horrible as it undoubtedly was, Joyce Parronage was the murderess of the seven men—the unconscious murderess, but still the murderess.

Having seen what I had seen, and heard what I had heard from her lips, I knew beyond all doubting that the soul of the witch-girl had been born again in the body of Joyce Parronage, typist. Nobody knew it but I. The soul of the witch-girl had slept until Joyce had come down to Graeme, her body so weak with illness and lack of sleep as to be unable to resist the savage spirit which had suddenly awakened to the call of the old familiar surroundings.

Her deep sleeps were easily explicable. I understood at once when she told me. She could not be aroused because she was dead inasmuch as her spirit had left her body. While her body lay in a deep trance, her spirit—the witch-girl's spirit—roamed the woods lusting for blood.

The solution was at once simple and difficult. She must go away. Once she left the neighbourhood I had reason to believe that the spirit would sleep again and forget; but the problem was to get her to go. It was obvious that she loved Donald—obvious, at any rate, to one who could read faces.

If he married her would she kill him the first night they were together, or would the spirit of the witch rest in peace? That was the problem I had to face. No one could have told, and I was fond of Donald, and did not like to risk it.

If they married and lived away from Graeme Hall they might achieve happiness; but the idea seemed too horrible. The best solution was for the girl to go as soon as possible, and for Donald to do his best to forget her. I determined to get Mrs Graeme to help me without telling her what I knew. There was no good to be gained by sharing my knowledge with her. She would either disbelieve me and laugh, or believe me and go mad. If I simply told her that I thought Miss Parronage quite unfit to be Donald's wife that would be quite sufficient. She would be very willing to aid me in finding some scheme to get her out of the neighbourhood.

But whatever was to be done would have to be done quickly.

I dressed very hurriedly for dinner that night in order to get in a word or two alone with Mrs Graeme. As I passed Donald's room I heard the scrape of his razor and knew that I had plenty of time. Mrs Graeme came down into the drawing-room before I had been there more than a minute.

'Well?' she said.

I knew what she meant, but for no particular reason affected not to understand.

'What do you think of Joyce?' she asked. 'No, don't say you think she's pretty; we all know that. You know what I want to ask you.'

'Mrs Graeme,' I said, 'there is a little problem that you and I have got to solve—how to get Miss Parronage out of the way without either herself or poor old Donald suspecting that we have had a hand in the business.'

Mrs Graeme looked closely at me. 'You don't like her,' she said 'It isn't a case of personal like and dislikes,' I answered quickly. 'I think we must save Donald from marrying her. '

'Ah!' she said, and nodded. And then, suddenly, 'Why?'

I shrugged my shoulders. 'You yourself thought she wasn't quite nice,' I answered. 'I don't think so, either. You know I am a pretty good judge of character and intention. I think it would be a bad thing for Donald if he married her. '

Heaven knows I had no wish to slander the poor girl, but in her own interests as well as Donald's I had to do it.

'I am glad to hear you say that,' she said. 'To tell you the truth I think she is just a scheming minx, with no love at all of Donald, but a strong ambition to be mistress here. I am not such a fool as to speak disparagingly of loveless marriages in general, but that state of things would not suit Donald. I believe it would kill him if he married her and found that his love was not returned. Besides, she is very nearly impossible socially.'

Had I been on Donald's side I should have retorted that women learn things very quickly, but as it was I accepted the additional argument without comment.

'Now comes the question of ways and means,' I said. 'Donald would never forgive me if he knew I had a hand in manoeuvring the girl out of his way. Heaven knows I wish I had no hand in this business. " 'Tis an awkward thing to play with souls, and matter enough to save one's own." '

'If there is to be any blame in Donald's eyes I will take it all,' Mrs Graeme answered. 'The boy would never cherish a grudge against his mother. But suppose we get her away from here at once, what is to prevent Donald from following?'

I was easy enough in my mind about that. There was no harm, so far as I could see, in Donald meeting the girl away from the neighbourhood of Graeme Hall. But Mrs Graeme and I were looking at the matter from different standpoints. All that concerned me was that Joyce should go away at once and stop away. I had really no prejudices against her except that single, terrible one.

'Oh,' I answered airily, 'Donald will soon forget her, so long as he does not suspect that obstacles are being purposely thrown in his way. He won't be able to leave Graeme just at present, either, with all these horrors going on.'

I could have bitten my tongue out for thus foolishly mentioning the one topic which Mrs Graeme could not bear to discuss. She went instantly white.

'Bill,' she whispered, sinking her voice as if afraid that some unseen person might hear, 'what do you think of all these horrors?'

I shook my head It would not have done to have shared my terrible suspicions with Donald's mother.

'They did not begin until she came down here,' Mrs Graeme continued; and at the words I looked away from her, but felt her eyes upon me. Next moment, however, she was speaking in an altered voice. 'No, no, that's a horrible thing to say,' she exclaimed. 'It is only because I dislike her. What could she have to do with it, poor child? I am afraid I am a terribly catty woman sometimes, Bill.'

'Let us return to the subject of how she is to be got rid of,' I said. 'If she is indeed anxious to catch Donald it may be difficult.'

'I think it can be done,' Mrs Graeme answered smiling. 'She is at least anxious about her health, and Dr Kelland, who is attending her down here, would do anything for me. He will tell her, if I ask him, that the air here is not quite strong enough, and send her to the seaside. So long as she is parted from Donald for a short while it will be all right. You can leave that to me. I will fill the house with the prettiest girls in the county and set myself seriously to the task of getting him married. '

I smiled to myself at this, but it was not for me to throw a damper over her plans. If Joyce Parronage could be got out of the neighbourhood for a time, that was at least something, and would give me thinking space.

Donald's appearance, almost simultaneous with the rattle of the gong, put an end to our talk, and we went in to dinner together.

Afterwards, when Mrs Graeme had gone to the drawing-room, leaving us together for a short smoke, Donald leaned across the table and addressed me excitedly.

'I say, Bill,' he cried, I've got something now that'll lay the ghost I've heard of the remedy before, but forgot all about it until I happened to glance at a chapter on daemonology in an old book. We're going to try it, you and I.' I did not take him very seriously at the time.

'Oh,' said I, 'what's your wonderful remedy? Holy water and garlic used to be considered the most efficacious.'

it's neither of those,' he answered. 'Part of the paraphernalia is up in my bedroom, and the other part I've left in the gun-room. I'll show you when the mater's gone to bed.'

I did not put any further questions, since it pleased Donald to be mysterious. He knew nothing of things psychical, and seemed childishly pleased at something he had done or meant to do. I did not bother to cross-examine him then and there, for I had plenty to think about. We sat smoking in silence until Donald suddenly got up and said that Mrs Graeme would be annoyed with us if we did not join her in the drawing-room.

The events of that evening, even to the smallest details, are all clear to the eye of my memory. In the drawing-room we were a silent and not a very cheerful trio. I had tried to do everything for the best, and in spite of this solace to my conscience I felt almost as if I had betrayed poor Donald in that I was plotting to part him from the girl he loved. To interfere with other people's love affairs, even with the best of intentions, is a thankless business, for one risks the loss of friendships, and the eternal question, is it my business, after all?' keeps repeating itself in one's ears.

Mrs Graeme was no happier than I. She loved her son, and knew that he must suffer before he could be cured. There was also a restraint between her and me, for neither of us knew all the other's reasons for being anxious to separate Donald from Joyce Parronage. Afterwards I learned that she had some faint suspicion of the dreadful thing I knew. Donald was aware that there was some shadow between us, and we were both thankful when she went to bed.

'Have a whisky?' he said when we were alone. 'Half a moment, and I'll go and get it myself. And I'm going to show you something. '

He was absent for about five minutes, and when he came back I heard him set down something heavy in the hall before entering with the tray and glasses.

He set down the tray and went out into the hall, to return immediately, carrying a gun. It was a large, old-fashioned double-barrelled breech-loader.

'I found it this evening in an old lumber room,' he said. 'Now you see how I am going to lay the ghost, or devil, or whatever is the cause of all these horrors?'

I did not understand for the moment, and he rattled something in his pocket and produced a little handful of glistening pellets.

'These are silver bullets,' he said. 'I've had them melted down. Now do you see, Bill?'

I was on my feet at once.

'Look here, Donald,' I said sharply, 'you know nothing at all of the occult. For God's sake don't meddle. You've asked me down here to elucidate the trouble—leave it to me. You admit that I know at least a little, and I warn you solemnly to throw away the bullets and put that gun back where you found it. '

He looked at me in astonishment.

'My dear fellow,' he exclaimed, 'what is the matter with you? The book said that a ghost, demon, witch, or other evil spirit, being struck with a silver bullet will expire just as a man smitten by a leaden ball. The book may be wrong, but what harm can there be in trying?'

I was endeavouring to be calm, but the sweat was standing out in great drops on my forehead. How could I tell him why he must not use the bullets?

'I can't explain,' I said. 'I can only tell you that you may run yourself and others into dangers that you do not dream of. For God's sake listen to me, Donald!'

'Oh, blow the danger to myself!' he retorted. 'I'm not a shirker. And what harm can I do anyone else?' He broke out into a little laugh. 'I'm not such a bad shot as all that, you know.'

'You asked me down here to try to help you,' I said as quietly as I was able, 'and if you will be guided by me I will stand by you and see this thing through. But if you play the fool with charms and things you don't understand I will take the first train back to town tomorrow morning.'

Even then he hesitated. I could see that he was disappointed at the idea of net carrying out his experiment with the silver bullets. But I was very necessary to him then, and with a wry smile he dropped them into his pocket with a little chink.

'Have your own way, then,' he said rather impatiently. And then, in an altered tone: 'Don't leave me, will you, Bill, old chap?'

'Of course I won't,' I said. 'Let's go and play billiards.'

We played until bedtime.

I awoke in the small hours of the morning, with a clear consciousness of not having been aroused by anything. I was so wide awake that I knew that this was one of the intermittent attacks of insomnia to which I was sometimes subject. I therefore propped myself up in bed and gave myself over to my
thoughts.

My room was dark, but not so dark that I could not see the hands of my watch, which I pulled out from under my pillow. It was just before two o'clock. As I put the watch back a fear flashed into my mind, hesitated, rested there, and began to grow rapidly. I had not extracted any definite promise from Donald that he would not go down to the spinney with that gun and those infernal silver bullets. He had merely given me to understand that he had abandoned the intention. It would be like him to creep away quietly and say nothing about it until the morrow morning, when he would wear an air of apology and contrition, and make, in answer to my upbraidings, the reply that the thing was done now and could not be altered.

I could not rest in bed without first assuring myself that all was well. Donald's room was next to mine, and to find out would be only the work of a few moments. Accordingly I slipped into my dressing-gown, went round to his door, and knocked.

I got no answer, and with a rapidly beating heart opened the door a few inches and peered in. The room was empty, the bed had not been slept in.

For one moment rage and anxiety struggled together in my heart. I stood there on the threshold and damned him heartily. Two moments later I was back in my room scrambling into my clothes—the first garments that came to hand.

My partial toilet was a matter of only a few seconds. I scrambled into my dress trousers, thrust my arms into a tweed jacket, and covered over the incongruity with a long waterproof overcoat. Then I went down and let myself out of the rear of the house through the drawing-room windows.

Once in the open air I began to run. A breeze from the north-east ruffled the trees, and the night was quite chilly enough to aid one in the exercise. The moon was up, and showed bravely through the white wisps of clouds that swam across her path. In the intervals when she was altogether clear of them, the whole landscape was varnished over with silver. One could see for miles.

I made for the spinney, which stood out black against the pale sky. The edge was fringed with shadow so dark that it daunted the eyes. I could not tell that the shadow concealed Donald; I did not know it until I was within half a dozen yards of him.

He was lying flat on his chest on the grass, a gun to his shoulder. He lay so still that at first I was frightened, because he made no movement at my approach. His name was on my tongue when I saw something that froze me and held me to silence—something inside the spinney.

A form, only distinct because of its whiteness, showed itself in the darkness of the trees. It flashed into view and out again, coming from behind a tree-trunk and then disappearing behind another. The gun followed it.

'Donald!' I cried, finding my voice at last.

I sprang towards him. The white shape showed itself again, and simultaneously the silence of the night was smashed and lacerated by the report of the gun. A long stream of flame lit up the night with yellow for the fraction of a moment. The white shape vanished like the flame of a candle puffed out by the wind.

I stood over Donald trembling.

'What have you done!' I cried. 'You fool—what have you done?'

He got upon his legs. At the sight of my face—its pallor and the horror that must have been written upon it—he began to laugh nervously.

'I think I've rid us of this infernal pest,' he said. 'Bill, did you see?'

I did not answer him. I knew that on the morrow morning Joyce Parronage would be found dead in her bed with a silver bullet in her heart. Pity for him, and the shock of this culminating tragedy, baffled me of speech.

It was not I who told Donald what he had done; but he learned next day.

**'Orders from Brigade'**

I met Kesdaile down at Shoreham Camp towards the end of the summer of '18. The London and Eastern Command Depots were there then, facing each other across the narrow, chalky road that leads to Bramber. We were about ten thousand strong, all flotsam of the Great War, men out of hospitals and convalescent homes, passing through the machinery which purposed making soldiers of us again.

We were all jostled together in numbered companies, irrespective of our regiments, and graded according to our physical fitness. One began in Group Six, 'the Creeping Barrage' it was called, whose only duty was to parade at half-past ten in loose dress, shuffle two hundred yards or so at a snail's pace, and lie down in the sun for an hour on that pleasant ridge of the downs which looks out over the winding, tidal waters of the Adur to the chapel of Lancing College.

It was as good a time as men in the ranks could ever hope to enjoy. For the first few weeks we were encouraged to be lazy, and our frayed nerves responded to the treatment, so that we did not cry out quite so often in our sleep and looked out less haggardly upon the future. After tea we were free until midnight to go where we pleased within certain limits, and we made out our own passes to Brighton and Worthing, which were automatically stamped in Company Office.

In those days there was a Y.M.C.A. close to the station, run by local ladies, where one could get quite a reasonably good cup of tea for a penny, war-time cakes for the same modest sum, and sit in comfort at a table to look at the back numbers of the illustrated journals. I used to hobble down there most afternoons and rest for half an hour or so until the Brighton or Worthing train was nearly due; and it was there that I fell into conversation with Kesdaile for the first time.

I had seen him before, for although we were not in the same hut we were both in Number Ten Company and both members of 'the Creeping Barrage'.

For reasons which will later become apparent I cannot mention the name of his regiment, but his battalion had belonged 'over there' to a division which frequently lay alongside mine. We found ourselves at the same table one afternoon, and naturally got talking. I forget what we talked about at first, but I know that I was delighted to find him intelligent and amusing, besides owning a certain not unpleasant reserve.

Thomas Atkins—if I may be allowed to criticise my brother Thomases of those days—was the finest chap in the world, but his ideas were few and his conversation limited. I got on with him very well, but I grew tired of his pet topics, and mine would have bored him to distraction.

Kesdaile, I think, had been in the same boat He was younger than I—not more than twenty-three, I should think—and he was cultured rather than well educated. He had found time to read things, and we had much the same outlook on life—or, rather, I suppose, we had the same curiosity to get beneath the surface of things and surprise Truth at the bottom of her well.

Of course, we became friends, and we met most evenings and went out together. We were both amply supplied with pocket money, and we dined together as luxuriously as possible in those days of ration cards and meat tickets. So it happened that it was in the Pier Hotel at Worthing, between nine and ten on a wet, August night, that he told me the story of Jimmy Leeds.

It may be remembered that stories of psychic experiences were very much in the air in those days. Women were writing to the papers to state that they had seen their sons or husbands at the precise moment when these had been killed over in France. I was inclined to pooh-pooh it all. God knows, women suffered enough in those days to be forgiven a thousand delusions each. Kesdaile was more guarded in his attitude and said that he wouldn't like to call an apparition necessarily a delusion merely because it was subjective.

'If anything were needed,' I continued, 'to explode the ghost myth, the War has done that effectually. Look at the ground we've covered out there, where literally millions of men on both sides have been killed. But apart from the Angels of Mons—for which we have to thank Mr Arthur Machen in the first place—has the Western Front produced anything at all like a ghost story? The whole line from the coast to Switzerland ought to be stiff with ghosts if such things could exist.'

Kesdaile smiled only very faintly.

'Oh, yes,' he said, 'there was the ghost of the traffic man on the Menin Road, who used to turn the troops back before Jerry started shelling.'

'I never heard of him,' I returned, 'but I'd like to bet he drew pay and rations like the rest of us. Did you ever meet anybody who saw him?'

'No, but I met fellows who said they knew men who had.'

'It's always the way!' I laughed.

'I just about half believe in him,' Kesdaile admitted. 'Perhaps he neglected his duty in life'

'In that case,' I said, 'there'll be shadowy quartermaster-sergeants dishing out rum for all eternity every few hundred yards from the Belgian Coast to St Quentin.'

He chuckled reminiscently.

'But I wish you wouldn't laugh,' he said. 'I'd had half a mind to tell you something, but I won't now.'

'I won't laugh if you're really serious,' I promised.

'It isn't any laughing matter to me. I knew the fellow well—Jimmy Leeds his name was—and when I got back to Blighty he came into all my nightmares. I expect you had 'em, too, when you first got back. Anyhow, this actually happened. There can't be more than three living men besides myself who know anything about it, and perhaps two of those are only left guessing. There's no getting away from it at all. Either I'm a liar or else the thing happened.'

I looked straight into his eyes, and a little more coolly perhaps than was altogether polite.

'No,' I said after a pause, 'I don't think you're a liar. If I don't believe you it will be because I think you've been deluded in some way. Anyhow, I promise not to laugh. '

He touched my sleeve.

'Come and sit down in the comer, then—two bitters, please, miss—and I'll tell you. It's a bit of a long story, and I'm afraid, if you don't mind, I shall have to begin at the beginning. '

And this is Kesdaile's story, nearly exactly as he told it.

Jimmy Leeds was a private in my own platoon, young and happy-go-lucky and a good sort, popular with pretty well everybody. He was well educated, and a cut above most of the rest of us. He'd have had a commission, only he'd got on the carpet before we went out for pinching leave or something. Well, one's crime sheet is washed out directly one goes overseas, and about this time last year he was sweating on a commission once more, and expecting any day to go up before the Brigadier.

We were holding the line in front of Arras at the time, the sector was as quiet as you could expect a sector to be, and we ought to have been having a picnic. About twice a day a shell would sail over on to Arras and give the poor old cathedral another crack, and occasionally he used to bump our supports to let us know he was still there, and chuck over an odd Minnie or two at night; and that was about all that was happening. The weather was perfect, too—much too perfect considering we had to go about three miles to get water. But on the whole we ought to have been having a pretty good time, and we should have had but for the Staff. The Staff made it hell.

The trouble was that the sector was so quiet that we were doing sixteen days in the trenches and eight out—and 'out' only meant going to so-called rest in some insanitary old dug-outs in the railway cutting, where we were just in front of our own guns and naturally got sloshed worse than when we were in the line. Our cooks weren't with us. The little cooking *they* did was done in St Catherine's, and the rations came up at night in railway trucks which the transport fellows had to shove. It took about all night to get 'em from the front line, and then we had to do a lot of our own cooking. Certainly we had to make our own tea, and it took about two hours to boil a mess-tin full on the kind of Tommy Cookers which the Drums were making and sending up to us.

There were no dug-outs, and as they stopped us from making funk-holes there was nowhere to lie down on the rare occasions when we were allowed to rest. If you lay at the bottom of the trench somebody came and trod on you. All we could do was to sit on the fire-step and try to lean a little sideways.

There was no earthly chance of sleep of a night. We were either doing sentry or getting rations or out wiring or doing some other job of work. After stand-to in the mornings we had to clean up for inspection, and after that we were allowed to have breakfast. That took us a dickens of a while, as I've explained. And just as we were falling asleep on our feet the Brigadier or the Brigade-Major would come round with some of the junior staff—beautiful lads in primrose-coloured bags—fresh from a good meal and a clean bed in some safe dug-out behind the lines. It was a quiet spot and fine weather, as I've told you, so they came round every day—and, of course, they couldn't endure the sight of fagged-out men trying to rest. 'Can't you find these men something to do, Captain Ridgeway?'—that always came next.

So those of us who weren't due almost at once to go on sentry would be dragged off on some absurd and unnecessary working-party—carting duckboards to a place where they weren't wanted and then bringing them back again. Our officers were decent enough, but they couldn't help themselves. For sixteen days and nights on end I've never lain down once nor slept for more than an hour at a time. Never at any other place or time have I endured such mental agony through lack of sleep. We've both been through far worse in other ways, I know, and it seems so childish merely to talk of being tired—unless the other fellow's been through it, too.

Half of us walked in our sleep when we ever got any, and talked rot and did idiotic things, we were in such a state. And then they wondered why men fell asleep on sentry! I suppose no numb-skulled court martial has ever asked itself how it is possible for a man to go to sleep on his hind legs, knowing that his life is doubly in danger, unless he's actually at the end of his tether and nature's got too strong for him. As a matter of fact, I don't think they did shoot many fellows for that; only just now and again to make examples. Most of us ought to have copped it, anyway, for any number, I among them, were caught by our own officers who very sportingly woke us up and pretended not to notice. *They* knew what our sufferings were like.

The worst time for that was the daytime. Fellows didn't fall asleep at night, standing up and looking over the top. They'd have fallen off the fire-step if they had. Besides, the night was the dangerous time, and fellows were keyed up more. But looking for two hours on end in bright sunshine at a bit of looking-glass stuck at an angle on the top of a bayonet, when you could hardly keep your eyes open, and staring at the reflection of coarse grass and poppies stirring in the wind—that was simply maddening. It was just like looking into the eyes of a hypnotist.

Well, to come to the crux of things, one morning when we'd been in the trenches about twelve days, the Brigade-Major came round and found poor old Jimmy Leeds standing before a periscope with his eyes closed. There was hell to pay, of course, and our skipper was powerless to save poor Jimmy. He was a good and a keen soldier was Jimmy, and quite fearless, but that didn't help him. He was put under arrest at once. I heard he cried when the C O. nagged him for letting the battalion down. Anyhow, away he went, and we didn't see him again.

What happened to him none of us knew—not the men, at any rate, for nothing came through about it in Part Two Orders. There were the usual rumours that he'd been shot, and that a firing-party from one mob had refused to do it and they'd had to fish up a firing-party from some other crowd—all the usual sort of stuff. But I never believed it at the time. I thought he was either doing Field Punishment somewhere, or else he'd got off altogether.

The mere fact that he hadn't come back meant nothing. When a man left the battalion you never knew when you'd see him again. Jimmy might have been pushed into some other battalion, or gone sick, or clicked for a soft job at the Base. I couldn't imagine them shooting old Jimmy Leeds who was such a good sort and who'd been so upset at being told that he'd let the battalion down. The ragging he'd had and the fact that he'd done in his second and last chance of a commission ought to have been punishment enough.

Well, that little spell in the line confirmed what I'd often thought before—that being a fire-step man, and a bomber at that, was an overrated pastime. I was well in with our sergeant-major, and as soon as there was a job going as a runner I got it.

After Arras we were moved over to Ypres and had a smack at Passchendaele. We were supposed to cross a river which wasn't there and take concrete pill-boxes bristling with machine-guns at the point of the bayonet. There weren't many of us left after that, and by the time we were back to about half strength again with fresh drafts we were panicked up to Cambrai to help prevent Jerry getting halfway to Paris after our much-advertised victory. Then we were shifted again, and when the show of March '18 began we were about half-way between Cambrai and Peronne.

It's funny how we soon forgot Jimmy Leeds and stopped talking about him and wondering what had happened. Yet not so funny, for death and disaster were such old friends and near neighbours that the fate of one man didn't make much of a topic of conversation. Besides, by March there were damned few in the crowd who knew him. I don't suppose there were more than three men left in A Company who were with us last year at Arras, and it goes without saying that there weren't any officers. And I wasn't with the Company at all—I was a runner attached to battalion headquarters.

I rather liked B.H.Q., except that I was under the eye of the C O. all the time. We had a new C O. after Cambrai, not one of our own officers, but a regular. He was a gentleman, a brave man and a good soldier, but he had no initiative. He wouldn't do the least thing without orders from Brigade. He might have been own brother to the boy who stood on the burning deck. And he rather specialised in issuing dramatic orders.

We had a devil of a time on that March retreat, just before I got my packet, but not so bad as they got it on our right. We lost our transport, of course, and had to do our fighting on empty tummies. It was one long series of rearguard actions. We kept on going back and going back, and just as we thought we were going to get a breather at last, Jerry would be bang on top of us again. Where Brother Boche got his men from beats me. The Somme was simply stiff with them.

I can't tell you the exact date when this happened, but it must have been the night after Peronne had fallen, or perhaps the night after that. Bapaume, you remember, held out a few days longer. There was a big gap on our right, and stragglers from another division which had been holding that bit of ground passed through us. We were all right on our left, but our right flank was in the air, and it was odds on that we'd be surrounded after dark.

We were then holding a line of old trenches in front of a village which the men called Doo Soo. Heaven knows what its real name was, but if I got a look at a map I might be able to find it. About a mile behind Doo Soo there was a system of trenches called the Cadoma Line. Brigade headquarters was in a village about a mile behind that. Telephone communication, of course, simply didn't exist, and early in the afternoon the C.O. sent me with a note to Brigade—to ask for instructions, I suppose.

There wasn't much left of Doo Soo after the first battle of the Somme, and I don't know how it came to have one brick left intact after what it went through that afternoon and evening. I didn't waste any time in going through it, I can tell you. You couldn't count the shell-bursts; there were so many, and directly you tried you were baffled by fresh ones bobbing up. There were brickbats as well as lumps of shrapnel flying about all over the place, and more than once I saw a whole wall in front of me vanish in a great black cloud.

But if I didn't like going I hated it worse coming back. Doo Soo was ominously quiet, and I was in a morbid enough state of mind to suppose that this meant that Fritz was moving his guns. Of course, I didn't know what was in the chit I'd got from the Brigadier, but it was fairly obvious a little later. The C.O. issued one of his dramatic orders which went round to all four companies. Nobody was to retire or surrender, we were to stand where we were and hold our ground to the last man.

I don't pretend to know anything about tactics or strategy, but to my humble intelligence it seemed madness, with that gap on our right. I dare say another division was supposed to be coming up to fill it, but whether it came or not it wouldn't have come in time to save us from being mopped up. Everything was quiet until darkness fell, and then the strafing started. The shells came from our right flank, and from a slight angle in our rear, which wasn't comforting. I felt that we were all done for, but I'd felt like that so often, and somehow we'd always managed to wriggle through. Funny how one didn't get actually frightened; it was just a sort of mixture of depression and fatalism. Anyhow, I didn't see any chance for us where we were, and I knew that dynamite wouldn't budge our C O. once he'd got his orders.

Just after it got dusk I was sent with a message to one of the companies in the front line. I ran all the way with my head down and managed to dodge the torrents of five-nines which were coming over as thick as smoke out of an engine funnel. When I started back the shelling had stopped for a bit, and as I was fairly blown I didn't hurry. I'd got into the same line of trench in which B.H.Q. dug-out was situated, when I heard somebody hurrying behind me. I let him overtake me, and as he came round a traverse behind me into the same bay I turned my head and saw that it was Jimmy Leeds.

I don't think I was surprised. One soon lost the faculty of being surprised at anything out there, and just then I was incapable of any emotion. I merely said:

'Hallo, Jimmy, you've come back at the wrong time, haven't you?'

He didn't answer. He just pushed by me without a word, which wasn't like him. All the same, there was no mistake about it being Jimmy Leeds all right. His face was very grey and haggard, but then none of us was growing roses in his cheeks at that time. The odd thing was that he was wearing neither tin hat nor equipment nor gas-mask, and he didn't carry a rifle. Still, a lot of equipment and kit got lost on that retreat, and I remember thinking it just possible that he'd fallen into the hands of Jerry and managed to get away again.

Anyhow, he was in a tearing hurry, and I didn't try to stop him. If he were making for B.H.Q. dug-out, as I supposed he was, I should find him down there when I came to report myself back. About half a minute later a whizz-bang from our right flank came over my head like an express train and went up in a cloud on the parados not twenty yards behind me. That was the first of another small strafe, which lasted perhaps ten minutes. There was a hole close handy where somebody had started making a dug-out and hadn't got very far with the job, and I don't mind owning that I got into it and made myself as small as possible. During that time, though, I'll swear that Jimmy Leeds didn't pass me on his way back.

The shelling quietened, although it didn't altogether stop, and I went on again. B.H.Q. dug-out wasn't much of a one, and it was perilously shallow, being of British make. To get into it you had to slide down a short mud shaft on the seat of your bags, and to get out again you had to use your knees and elbows. I saw the adjutant going down just in front of me, and as I followed him a shell blew me right on top of him. When we had sorted ourselves out of the bottom I stood by until the adjutant had spoken to the C.O.

The C O. was standing up trying to read a map by the aid of a candle stuck in the neck of a bottle.

'Oh, Dickinson!' he cried, addressing the adjutant. 'I was just going to send for you when Kesdaile came back. I've just had orders. We retire on to the Cadoma Line immediately.'

I could have cheered, but, of course, I didn't. Captain Dickinson didn't look displeased, either.

'But,' he said, 'that directly contradicts what we had three hours ago.'

'I can't help that. The chit was perfectly in order. And it's the only sane thing to do now. They'll be on top of us any minute here.'

'Who brought it, sir?'

'Oh, one of our men! I could tell that by his numerals. I don't think I know him, though. He simply flew down here, stood at attention—he hadn't a hat, so he didn't salute—and handed it to me. I asked him where was his hat and the damn fellow didn't answer. I'd have told him something about that, but I was reading the chit and thinking of something else. And when I looked round the beggar was gone. Not so much as'

'Are you sure it was one of our men, sir?' the adjutant asked meaningly.

'Oh, yes, and the form was in perfect order—perfect order.'

'Could I see it, please, sir?' Captain Dickinson asked deferentially.

'Yes, of course—oh, damn it, what did I do with it? I had it in my hand just now. Now what the blazes—' He began to fumble in vain in his tunic pockets. 'Anyhow, I had it and it's in order.' He turned to me. 'Did you see one of our men without a hat just now?'

'Yes, sir.'

'Do you know him? Who was he?'

'Leeds, sir, of A Company.'

The adjutant looked mystified but the C O. said:

'Yes, yes! I know that name.'

'I beg pardon, sir,' I ventured, 'but he left the battalion before you came to us and he can only just have got back.'

'I know nothing about him,' said the adjutant.

The C.O. slammed down his map.

'Sent up from the Base, I s'pose, and Brigade snaffled him on the way to use as a runner. Damned feller! Why the blazes didn't he stop and explain himself! Now, Kesdaile, I want you. You're not to waste a single moment, do you understand?'

Well, we got out of that bit of line as quickly as a battalion ever did get out without actually haring for it. There was no other battalion to come and take over, and that expedited matters a good deal. We were lucky, too, for the strafing died down, and though we didn't waste any time getting through Doo Soo not a single shell fell on the place while we were in it. There was nobody in the place to warn, either, for the R.E.'s, pioneers, and other oddments who'd been living in the cellars, had already pushed off. And we got safely into the Cadoma Line and found quite first-rate trenches except that there was no wire in front.

We hadn't been settled very long, though, before the band began to play. We could see the bit of line which we'd left because it was beautifully picked out in the dark by the flashes of shell-bursts. Doo Soo was getting it well in the neck at the same time, but, of course, we didn't care how much of Fraulein Schmidt's war-loan Jerry wasted by bumping a smashed-up and deserted village. Little or nothing came over our way, except that, from time to time, one or two would drop on the road behind us leading to Brigade HQ.

After a hectic hour or two there was sudden peace once more, and the Old Man sent out a patrol to the outskirts of Doo Soo to see what was doing. The patrol came back, minus all its bombs and one man, and reported that Doo Soo was stiff with Jerries. We'd got out in the nick of time, and Jerry was left wondering where we were. And we knew that he wasn't going to take too many chances looking for us in the dark.

I couldn't help thinking all this time how queer it was that Jimmy Leeds, who'd been accused of letting the battalion down, should have come back just in time to save it; and I wondered where he'd got to.

In the small hours of the morning, up comes a composite battalion from the rear led by a Jock officer. Our fellows stopped them on the road, not knowing who they were, and they nearly opened fire on each other. The Jock officer was presently led down into B.H.Q. dug-out.

'Good Lord!' he says to our C.O. 'Are there any of you left?'

'Rather!' says our C.O. 'We're averaging sixty to a company, and that's pretty good in these hard times. '

'Splendid!' says the other. 'Well, from what your Brigadier found time to tell me we didn't expect to find you here or anywhere at all. I understood -' And then he lowered his voice.

Three or four days later the big push petered out, or, rather, it broke out in a new place. Another Division came up and relieved us, and we actually had four days' rest in a fairly civilised village, where we could buy eggs and *vin blanc* and where we actually had a pay parade.

Our C.O. had quite a decent billet in a good-sized farm, and one morning I was sitting in the kitchen, talking to his batman, when he called me into his office. He was quite alone, and he told me to stand easy and afterwards to sit down.

'Kesdaile,' he said, 'you're a sensible youngster and I think you can keep your mouth shut. I want to say something unofficial to you. First, have you seen anything lately of Private Leeds?'

'No, sir,' I answered, 'not since that evening in front of Doo Soo.'

'And he's not on the Battalion strength,' said the C.O., 'so you must have made a mistake. By the way, was he the man who was court-martialled back at the end of last summer for being found asleep on sentry?'

'Yes, sir.'

'Then it couldn't have been he. And the odd thing is—Look here, that order *didn't* come from Brigade, although Brigade sent out a similar one which didn't reach me. '

And he went on to tell me how, when it seemed much too late, a Brigade runner—one of those chaps with blue brassards—was found dead on the road beside a new shell-hole and a smashed-up motor-bike, with the message which he'd never lived to deliver still in his possession.

'And now,' continued the C O., 'I want to know who brought me what seems to have been an exact duplicate. It's a perfectly extraordinary business.'

'*Couldn't* it have been Private Leeds, sir?' I asked.

He looked at me very squarely for a moment.

'*That* Private Leeds,' he said, 'is dead. He was sentenced to death and shot last September. I happen to know and to remember the case, although I had nothing to do with the battalion at the time, because my nephew acted as his "friend" at the court martial.'

He looked at me very hard again and I felt myself go all over pins and needles.

'I shouldn't talk about it, and I shouldn't think about it much if I were you,' he said.

## A.M. Burrage – The Life And Times.

Alfred McLelland Burrage, better known as simply AM Burrage, was born in Hillingdon, Middlesex on July 1st, 1889, to Alfred Sherrington Burrage and Mary E. Burrage. On his Father's side writing already ran in the family's blood as both he and an uncle, Edwin Harcourt Burrage, were writers of the then very popular boys' magazine fiction.

Life in late Victorian times was by no means easy and writing has always been a precarious career for most. For an insight into the young AM and his surroundings it is interesting to see how certain facts were captured in the 1891 census when he was aged one. The family is listed as living at Uxbridge Common in Hillingdon. His father is 40 and his mother 36. In the next census of 1901, and with it the end of the Victorian era, the family has moved to 1 Park Villa, Newbury. In that time his father has aged 17 years his mother 6 years and young AM has disappeared from the records. It's almost a precursor to one of his stories.

There is little documented about his growing up and education. What we can glean though is something about his environment. His neighbours were varied: a tailor's journeyman, a corn porter, a lodging-house keeper and a grocer's assistant. Nothing particularly illustrious, so times cannot have been as rosy as they should, especially in the light of his Father's hard work. Alfred Sherrington wrote for The Boy's World, Our Boys' Paper, The Boys of England, and various others. He also appears to have written under the pseudonym Philander Jackson and edited The Boys' Standard and that one of his more celebrated pieces was a retelling of the story of Sweeney Todd entitled "The String of Peals; or, Passages from the Life of Sweeney Todd, the Demon Barber".

Sadly Alfred Sherrington Burrage died in 1906. There is a biographical note in Lloyd's Magazine, from 1921, which suggests that young Alfred McLelland was studying at St. Augustine's, the Catholic Foundation School in Ramsgate, and most probably away from home at the time.

A.M. Burrage was 16 years old when he had his first story published; the same year as his father's death, in the prestigious boys' paper, Chums. It was a great start to his professional career and whether doors had been opened by his father and family or not the young man's career now had to stand on its own. He was now primary provider for the household and this was the only way he could do it. His Mother, sister and aunt must be provided for.

Magazine fiction was his family's blood and business and for A. M. Burrage, business was good. He established himself as a competent and creative writer and was busy writing stories and articles on a weekly basis for publications such as Boys' Friend Weekly, Boys'

Herald, Comic Life, Vanguard, Dreadnought, Triumph Library Cheer Boys Cheer, and Gem, under the pseudonym 'Cooee'.

However, unlike his father and uncle who had remained firmly and easily categorised as boys' writers, he had his sights set on the more well regarded, more lucrative, adult market. Burrage was aided in his early years as a professional writer by Isobel Thorne of the off-Fleet Street publishing firm Shurey's. Her publications have been characterised as "low in price, modest in payments, but whose readers were avid for romance, thrills, sensation, strong characterisation and neat plotting", and this estimation of her publications also fits nicely the description of Burrage's own writing at that time. For a young writer this sort of readership was vital, and the modest wages he received were bolstered by the exposure the publications brought him. Burrage was certainly helped by Thorne's use of young writers.

At the time Burrage was beginning to really establish himself as a writer, the entire magazine fiction scene was benefiting from what we would now see as disruptive influences: new printing techniques, a growing readership with more disposable income and leisure time and other media failing to provide – though obviously movies and such were only in their infancy at the time. The market was lively and commercial, and the readership interested, excitable and willing to pay. P. G. Wodehouse, of Jeeves fame, recalls these years:

We might get turned down by the Strand, but there was always the hope of landing with Nash's, the Story-teller, the London, the Royal, the Red, the Yellow, Cassell's, the New, the Novel, the Grand, the Pall Mall, and the Windsor, not to mention Blackwood's, Cornhill, Chambers's and probably about a dozen more I've forgotten.

With War clouds darkening the skies of Europe in 1914 Burrage was firmly established as a magazine writer, securing publication in London Magazine and The Storyteller, which were both highly prestigious publications. Alongside he had plenty printed in less illustrious publications such as Short Stories Illustrated.

By now Burrage, a young man of twenty-four-year-was eligible for the Armed Services. Under the 'Derby Scheme' he confirmed that he was available for service if called upon in December 1915. Conscription was to follow shortly though, by that time, Burrage had already voluntarily enrolled in the Artists Rifles.

The significance of Burrage's decision to join the Artists Rifles is made clear by the nature of the unit itself. They formed in the middle of the nineteenth century, a group of volunteer artists comprising musicians, writers, painters and engravers. Minerva and Mars were their patrons, one of wisdom, arts, and defence, the other of war. The unit boasted several significant figures as ex-servicemen, including Dante Gabriel Rossetti, Algernon Charles Swinburne and William Morris. It was a popular unit with students and recent postgraduates, and the training was considered and extensive.

In Burrage's vivid, celebrated account of World War I entitled War is War, he insists that he was a volunteer and not a conscript, though as has already been noted, it is quite possible that his decision to join such a respected territorial unit may have been more of an effort to secure himself a more congenial army posting; had he waited for conscription, he would have had little choice over those with whom he was posted. Unlike poets Wilfred Owen or Edward Thomas, Burrage did not achieve a commission, and he suggests in War is War that this may be a result of his extremely unmilitary personality and his shortcomings as a soldier.

Add to this the fact that as the breadwinner for the family he was putting himself in harm's way. If anything were to happen to him the result on the family would be devastating. With the death of
Edwin Harcourt Burrage in 1916 it came even more starkly into focus.

Even though he was now a soldier he was still a writer and writers had to write. It also helped that it was a distraction from the mindless carnage around him. He experimented with various genres, excelling in the one that was to prove most lucrative for him; the light romance, in which a male character invariably meets a female character, there is a problem or hurdle to their being together, they overcome it and they live happily ever after. Burrage's talent for this formula was such that he could work seemingly endless minor variations from the same basic storyline and so he was able to keep writing a steady body of easy work.

He gives a fascinating account of the practicalities of writing such fiction during wartime in War is War, in which he remarks on the difficulties of censorship: "the problem of censorship was an acute one to me. It was well enough to write a story, but the difficulty was to get it censored. Officers were shy of tackling five thousand words or so, written in indelible pencil..." After some time he managed to find a chaplain who was willing to undertake the censorship. However, in order to secure this chaplain's favour and thus his services he was obliged to appear to be holy. Though he did so in earnest while he was with the chaplain, his efforts were dashed when the chaplain found him, sprawled on top of a young girl, and realised Burrage's piety to be a fraudulent con. As Burrage had anticipated, the reality of his behaviour ensured that this particular opportunity was swiftly ended. Resourceful to the last, though, he writes of his solution: "there were 'green envelopes' which could be sent away sealed and were liable only to censorship at the base, but these were only sparingly issued... I met an A.S.C. lorry driver who had stolen enough green envelopes to last me for the rest of the war; and since he only wanted two francs for them I was free of the censorship from that day forward."

Although we know that Burrage had his family to support at home as an incentive to keep writing, at times in War is War he reveals a more intimate aspect of his relationship with his work.

"It was a great relief to me to write when it was at all possible – to sit down and lose myself in that pleasant old world I used to know and pretend to myself that there never had been a war. Some of my editors seemed of the opinion that we were not suffering from one now. One used to write to me saying "Couldn't you let me have one of your light, charming love stories of country house life by next Thursday." I would get these letters in the trenches during the usual 'morning hate' when my fingers were too numb to hold a pencil, when I was worn out with work and sleeplessness, and when I was extremely doubtful if there ever would be another Thursday".

Writing is a useful therapy and for Burrage it provided a means to escape if only for a short time to a world that he could control and move at will.  With the misery and harsh conditions of the War dragging on he was eventually invalided and so he returned to England.

One of the best insights we have as to the character which Burrage presented on his return from the war is to be found in Lloyd's's 1920 publication of Captain Dorry, one of Burrage's story series. In that publication there was included a brief sketch of Burrage, describing his personality.

A.M. BURRAGE is the type of young man who might very well walk out of one of his own stories. He commenced yarn-spinning as a boy of fifteen at St Augustine's, Ramsgate, writing stories of school life to provide himself with pocket-money. Since then he has won his spurs as one of the most popular of magazine writers. Everything he does has charm and reflects his own romantic spirit – for he is incurably romantic and hopelessly lazy. It is his misfortune, although he would not admit it, that his work finds a too ready market. Nevertheless, his friends hope that one day he will wake up and do justice to himself. Otherwise he may end up as a "best-seller", a fate which doubtless he contemplates with equanimity.

Despite the sketch's fairly accurate but negative summation of Burrage's literary output up to that point, some of his stories seem to exhibit a desire to write about more than just his usual romantic plots. The most immediate change of this nature is in his decision to bring some of his wartime experience into his work, despite being perfectly aware that such writing was not at all what his editors desired, for they feared it would upset and intimidate their readership.

An example of this can be found in "A Town of Memories", published in 1919 in Grand Magazine, in which he uses his well rehearsed romantic story with a slight shift of emphasis to explore his own return from the war and the general reception which soldiers received on their return. Following a young officer as he returns to the town in which he grew up, Burrage portrays an almost hostile environment into which he returns; he is unrecognised, and nobody pays any interest, respect or attention to him or his stories of the war, nor even to his reception of the Distinguished Service Order. Instead, the people of the town have their own interests and priorities with which to concern themselves. Though this contentious portrayal of post-war society certainly marks a slight shift in Burrage's writing, he returns to the romantic convention expected of him by reuniting the officer with a beautiful girl who had admired him throughout school.  It would be harsh to not accept that market conditions expected one thing and to ignore them would mean turning his back on publications who still clamoured for his penmanship.

Another of Burrage's alternative directions is to be found in "The Recurring Tragedy", in which a  General whose war tactics of attrition had been to the slaughtered cost of his soldiers, and he comes to re-imagine his own past as a Judas figure in a terrible vision. The

Strange Career of Captain Dorry became a series for Lloyd's Magazine in 1920 about a gentleman crook and an ex-officer with a Military Cross who, idle in peacetime, meets a mysterious man called Fewgin whose business is in stolen goods and mind reading. Fewgin realises Dorry is a suitable candidate for recruitment into his gang of like-minded ex-military thieves, stealing only from "certain vampires who made money out of the war, and, by keeping up prices, are continuing to make money out of the peace". Again, in this motive, we see a glimpse of Burrage's own feelings on the war, as there is undoubtedly a bitterness towards those profiting from the suffering of others in such a manner. Fewgin justifies himself, saying:

"I help brave men who cannot help themselves. I give them a chance to get back a little of their own from the men who battened and fattened on them, who helped to starve their dependents while they were fighting, who smoked fat cigars in the haunts of their betters, and hoped the war might never end."

Burrage began to see slightly more success in the 1920s, achieving a couple of hard back publications entitled Some Ghost Stories and Poor Dear Esme. The latter, a comedy, concerns a boy who, for various reasons, is forced to disguise himself as a girl. Though these hard cover publications were a notable achievement, and one of which he was proud, the fact was that there was less money in it than in the magazines. In his history of the Strand Magazine, Reginald Pound portrays Burrage around this time, likening him to his equally prolific contemporary Herbert Shaw, considering them "two Bohemian temperaments that suffused and at times confused gifts from which more was expected than come forth. They had a precise knowledge of the popular short story as the product of calculated design. Both privately despised it, though it was their living."

The early 1920s, and with them a boom in prosperity, hope and happiness, now brought with them an increase in demand for war stories. Rather than preferring to ignore the atrocities of the war, which had seemed the general attitude in the immediate post-war years, society became more interested and concerned with the manner in which the war was fought, and the greed and political battles which had necessitated such bloodshed. Burrage answered this demand in 1930 with his own epochal piece, War Is War. He published under the pseudonym 'Ex-Private X', saying "were it otherwise I could not tell the truth about myself", though its publisher, Victor Gollancz, "who published the book and greatly admired it, had to point out that the critics would hardly take the book seriously if it became known that the author earned his living producing two or three slushy love stories a week".

In one of a series of letters he wrote to his contemporary and fellow writer Dorothy Sayers, Burrage bemoans how War is War "promised to be a great success, but was only a moderate one". The book itself was received with reviews on both sides of the spectrum. Cyril Fall's War Books, a survey of post-war writing published in 1930, gives a clear indication as to why the critics were so mixed in reception of the book. He writes:

This book is extremely uneven in quality. The account of the attack at Paschendaele and of conditions at Cambrai after the great German counter-attack are very good indeed; in fact among the best of their kind. But the rest is disfigured by an unreasoned and unpleasant attack on superiors and all troops other than those of the front line, which is all the more astonishing because the author is inclined to harp upon his social position as compared with that of many of the officers with whom he came in contact. He does not use as much bad language as many writers on the War, but his methods of abuse will leave on some of his readers at least a worse impression than the most highly-spiced language.

Dorothy Sayers was the editor at Victor Gollanz for anthologies of ghost and horror stories which included stories by Burrage. She says, in one of her letters of Burrage's story The Waxwork, a piece beyond the nerves of the editors, "what you say about "The Waxwork" sounds very exciting, just the sort of thing I want. Our nerves are stronger than those of the editors of periodicals, and we will publish anything, so long as it does not bring us into conflict with the Home Secretary". Though their correspondence began as strictly business, Burrage's acquaintance with Atherton Fleming, Sayers's husband, allowed their interactions to become less formal and friendlier. Burrage wrote of Fleming "I hope to encounter him soon in one of the Fleet Street tea-shops". 'Tea-shop' being a popular euphemism for the pub, where both Burrage and Fleming could frequently be found, though their alcohol consumption came to damage both their health and their professions, with Burrage coming off the worse.

Happily for Burrage, as a result of being featured in one of Sayers's anthologies, The Waxwork became one of his best-known stories and it would grab the attention of the film companies several times down the years even becoming an episode in the TV series 'Alfred Hitchcock Presents'.

The developing friendship between Burrage and Sayers enabled him to reveal more details of his personal life, admitting to her his "neuritis at both ends (legs and eyes)", and hinting at his troubles with alcohol: "Fleet Street is not a good place for a man who delights in succumbing to temptation, and whose doctor says that even small doses of alcohol are poison to him". Sayers sympathises, replying that Fleming "agrees with you entirely about the temptations of Fleet Street; he has, however, succeeded, through sheer strength of character, in being able to drink soda-water in the face of all his fellow journalists".

In another of Burrage's letters, he apologises for a delay in sending proofs of a story, with the words:

I have had a pretty thin time lately through illness and anxiety. And for days on end haven't had the energy in me to write a letter, and when I had the energy to send a complete set of proofs to you I found I hadn't the postage money (This is when you take out your handkerchief and start sobbing). I owed my late agent over £1000, so I got practically nothing out of War is War. He stuck to it. Well, he is paid off now, and so are my arrears of income tax. All this took a toll of my very small earning capacity, and I have been sold up. This on top of something which promised to be a great success and was only a moderate one, was a bit too much for me. Still, in spite of sickness I am resilient and shall float again. "You can't keep a good man down," as the whale said about Jonah.

For a man who had so many stories in so many magazines, and was gaining pace in Sayers's anthologies as a talented writer of horror stories, his income will have been far higher than the then average wage, and yet as he says, he finds himself short of money.

Several questions are left unanswered about his personal life. It is unclear whether he was still supporting family, or whether he spent the majority of his money on alcohol, or whether he chose to conceal his true fortunes from those around him. Perhaps most incongruous is the apparent absence of a wife; though his death certificate indicates that he had one, listed as H.A. Burrage, he seems never to mention her to Sayers.

He was around forty-two when he wrote that apology letter to Sayers, though in tone and circumstance it seems to be from a man in a far later stage of his life.

Burrage continued writing until his death in 1956, and continued to be prolifically published. Indeed, the Evening News alone published some forty of his stories between 1950-56. His death is recorded at Edgware General Hospital on 18th December, and the causes of his death are recorded as congestive cardiac failure, arteriosclerosis and chronic bronchitis. He was sixty-seven years old, and his last address is listed as 105 Vaughan Road, Harrow.

Though his name is not often remembered in lists of prominent writers of his time, or even it's genres, his ghost stories are highly regarded by critics and fans alike, while his life story tells us much about the trials and stresses placed on authors during and after the war, and on soldiers returning from that war. His reluctant acceptance that the money was in the magazines while the esteem was in the poorly-paying hard covers, and his persistence as a writer, speak of a determined man, doomed to circumstance yet living as best he could.

In ending A.M Burrage wrote a few sentences which best sum up two things. Firstly his love for his son Simon (who sadly passed away in October 2013 and was a great and passionate advocate for his Father's works.) and secondly his succinct reasons for writing.

TO JULIAN SIMON FIELD BURRAGE
who at the moment of writing will
soon achieve the great age of four.
From somebody who loves him.


In War is War I admitted being a professional writer, or in other words one who depends for his bread and cheese and beer on writing, typing or dictating strings of sentences which his masters, the Public, are kind enough to buy and presumably to read.

The book brought me letters from a few old friends and a great many new ones. A large percentage of the new friends, who missed having seen that my identity was rather unkindly betrayed by the Press, wrote and asked (a) who I was and (b) what sort of stories did I write?

The answer to the second question will be found in the following pages. The answer to the first question is 'Nobody Much', worse luck.

Most of these stories were written with the intention of giving the reader a pleasant shudder, in the hope that he will take a lighted candle to bed with him—for candle-makers must be considered in these hard times. Some have already made their bow from the pages of the monthly magazines. The best have, quite naturally, been rejected.